WILDERNESS WAYS

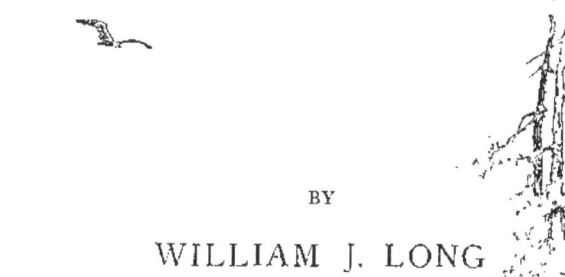

BY
WILLIAM J. LONG

SECOND SERIES

TO KILLOOLEET, Little Sweet-Voice, who shares my camp and makes sunshine as I work and play

PREFACE.

THE following sketches, like the "Ways of Wood Folk," are the result of many years of personal observation in the woods and fields. They are studies of animals, pure and simple, not of animals with human motives and imaginations.

Indeed, it is hardly necessary for genuine interest to give human traits to the beasts. Any animal is interesting enough as an animal, and has character enough of his own, without borrowing anything from man — as one may easily find out by watching long enough.

Most wild creatures have but small measure of gentleness in them, and that only by instinct and at short stated seasons. Hence I have given both sides and both kinds, the shadows and lights, the savagery as well as the gentleness of the wilderness creatures.

It were pleasanter, to be sure, especially when you have been deeply touched by some exquisite bit of animal devotion, to let it go at that, and to carry with you henceforth an ideal creature.

But the whole truth is better — better for you, better for children — else personality becomes confused with mere animal individuality, and love turns to instinct, and sentiment vaporizes into sentimentality.

This mother fox or fish-hawk here, this strong mother loon or lynx that to-day brings the quick moisture to your eyes by her utter devotion to the little helpless things which great Mother Nature gave her to care for, will to-morrow, when they are grown, drive those same little ones with savage treatment into the world to face its dangers alone, and will turn away from their sufferings thereafter with astounding indifference.

It is well to remember this, and to give proper weight to the word, when we speak of the *love* of animals for their little ones.

I met a bear once — but this foolish thing is not to be imitated — with two small cubs following at her heels. The mother fled into the brush; the cubs took to a tree. After some timorous watching I climbed after the cubs, and shook them off, and put them into a bag, and carried them to my canoe, squealing and appealing to the one thing in the woods that could easily have helped them. I was ready enough to quit all claims and to take to the brush myself upon inducement. But the mother had found a blueberry patch and was stuffing herself industriously.

And I have seen other mother bears since then, and foxes and deer and ducks and sparrows, and almost all the wild creatures between, driving their own offspring savagely away. Generally the young go of their own accord as early as possible, knowing no affection but only dependence, and preferring liberty to authority; but more than once I have been touched by the sight of a little one begging piteously to be fed or just to stay, while the mother drove him away impatiently. Moreover, they all kill their weaklings, as a rule, and the burdensome members of too large a family. This is not poetry or idealization, but just plain animal nature.

As for the male animals, little can be said truthfully for their devotion. Father fox and wolf, instead of caring for their mates and their offspring, as we fondly imagine, live apart by themselves in utter selfishness. They do nothing whatever for the support or instruction of the young, and are never suffered by the mothers to come into the den, lest they destroy their own little ones. One need not go to the woods to see this; his own stable or kennel, his own dog or cat will be likely to reveal the startling brutality at the first good opportunity.

An indiscriminate love for all animals, likewise, is not the best sentiment to cultivate toward creation. Black snakes in a land of birds, sharks in the bluefish rips, rabbits in Australia, and weasels everywhere are out of place in the present economy of nature. Big owls and hawks, representing a yearly destruction of thousands of good game birds and of untold innocent songsters, may also be profitably studied with a gun sometimes instead of an opera-glass. A mink is good for nothing but his skin; a red squirrel — I hesitate to tell his true character lest I spoil too many tender but false ideals about him all at once.

The point is this, that sympathy is too true a thing to be aroused falsely, and that a wise discrimination, which recognizes good and evil in the woods, as everywhere else in the world, and which loves the one and hates the other, is vastly better for children, young and old, than the blind sentimentality aroused by ideal animals with exquisite human propensities. Therefore I wrote the story of Kagax, simply to show him as he is, and so to make you hate him.

In this one chapter, the story of Kagax the Weasel, I have gathered into a single animal the tricks and cruelties of a score of vicious little brutes that I have caught red-handed at their work. In the other chapters I have, for the most part, again searched my old notebooks and the records of wilderness camps, and put the individual animals down just as I found them.

WM. J. LONG.

STAMFORD, September, 1900.

CONTENTS.

		PAGE
I.	MEGALEEP THE WANDERER	1
II.	KILLOOLEET, LITTLE SWEET-VOICE	26
III.	KAGAX THE BLOODTHIRSTY	41
IV.	KOOKOOSKOOS, WHO CATCHES THE WRONG RAT	59
V.	CHIGWOOLTZ THE FROG	75
VI.	CLOUD WINGS THE EAGLE	88
VII.	UPWEEKIS THE SHADOW	108
VIII.	HUKWEEM THE NIGHT VOICE	133

GLOSSARY OF INDIAN NAMES . . . 155

WILDERNESS WAYS.

I. MEGALEEP THE WANDERER.

MEGALEEP is the big woodland caribou of the northern wilderness. His Milicete name means The Wandering One, but it ought to mean the Mysterious and the Changeful as well. If you hear that he is bold and fearless, that is true; and if you are told that he is shy and wary and inapproachable, that is also true. For he is never the same two days in succession. At once shy and bold, solitary and gregarious; restless as a cloud, yet clinging to his feeding grounds, spite of wolves and hunters, till he leaves them of his own free will; wild as Kakagos the raven, but inquisitive as a blue jay,—he is the most fascinating and the least known of all the deer.

One thing is quite sure, before you begin your study: he is never where his tracks are, nor anywhere near it. And if after a season's watching and following you catch one good glimpse of him, that is a good beginning.

I had always heard and read of Megaleep as an awkward, ungainly animal, but almost my first glimpse of him scattered all that to the winds and set my nerves a-tingling in a way that they still remember. It was on a great chain of barrens in the New Brunswick wilderness. I was following the trail of a herd of caribou one day, when far ahead a strange clacking sound came ringing across the snow in the crisp winter air. I ran ahead to a point of woods that cut off my view from a five-mile barren, only to catch breath in astonishment and drop to cover behind a scrub spruce. Away up the barren my caribou, a big herd of them, were coming like an express train straight towards me. At first I could make out only a great cloud of steam, a whirl of flying snow, and here and there the angry shake of wide antlers or the gleam of a black muzzle. The loud clacking of their hoofs, sweeping nearer and nearer, gave a snap, a tingle, a wild exhilaration to their rush which made one want to shout and swing his hat. Presently I could make out the individual animals through the cloud of vapor that drove down the wind before them.

They were going at a splendid trot, rocking easily from side to side like pacing colts, power, grace, tirelessness in every stride. Their heads were high, their muzzles up, the antlers well back on heaving shoulders. Jets of steam burst from their nostrils at every bound; for the thermometer was twenty below zero, and the air snapping. A cloud of snow whirled out and up behind them; through it the antlers waved like bare oak boughs in the wind; the sound of their hoofs was like the clicking of mighty castanets —"Oh for a sledge and bells!" I thought; for Santa Claus never had such a team.

So they came on swiftly, magnificently, straight on to the cover behind which I crouched with nerves thrilling as at a cavalry charge, — till I sprang to my feet with a shout and swung my hat; for, as there was meat enough in camp, I had small wish to use my rifle, and no desire whatever to stand that rush at close quarters and be run down. There was a moment of wild confusion out on the barren just in front of me. The long swinging trot, that caribou never change if they can help it, was broken into an awkward jumping gallop. The front rank reared, plunged, snorted a warning, but were forced onward by the pressure behind. Then the leading bulls gave a few mighty bounds which brought them close up to me, but left a clear space for the frightened, crowding animals behind. The swiftest shot ahead to the lead; the great herd lengthened out from its compact mass; swerved easily to the left, as at a word of command; crashed through the fringe of evergreen in which I had been hiding,—out into the open again with a wild plunge and a loud cracking of hoofs, where they all settled into their wonderful trot again, and kept on steadily across the barren below.

That was the sight of a lifetime. One who saw it could never again think of caribou as ungainly animals.

Megaleep belongs to the tribe of Ishmael. Indeed, his Latin name, as well as his Indian one, signifies The Wanderer; and if you watch him a little while you will understand perfectly why he is called so. The first time I ever met him in summer, in strong contrast to the winter herd, made his name clear in a moment. It was twilight on a wilderness lake. I was sitting in my canoe by the inlet, wondering what kind of bait to use for a big trout which lived in an eddy behind a rock, and which disdained everything I offered him. The swallows were busy, skimming low, and taking the young mosquitoes as they rose from the water. One dipped to the surface near the eddy. As he came down I saw a swift gleam in the depths below. He touched the water; there was a swirl, a splash — and the swallow was gone. The trout had him.

Then a cow caribou came out of the woods onto the grassy point above me to drink. First she wandered all over the point, making it look afterwards as if a herd had passed. Then she took a sip of water by a rock, crossed to my side of the point, and took a sip there; then to the end of the point, and another sip; then back to the first place. A nibble of grass, and she waded far out from shore to sip there; then back, with a nod to a lily pad, and a sip nearer the brook. Finally she meandered a long way up the shore out of sight, and when I picked up the paddle to go, she came back again. Truly a *Wandergeist* of the woods, like the plover of the coast, who never knows what he wants, nor why he circles about so, nor where he is going next.

If you follow the herds over the barrens and through the forest in winter, you find the same wandering, unsatisfied creature. And if you are a sportsman and a keen hunter, with well established ways of trailing and stalking, you will be driven to desperation a score of times before you get acquainted with Megaleep. He travels enormous distances without any known object. His trail is everywhere; he is himself nowhere. You scour the country for a week, crossing innumerable trails, thinking the surrounding woods must be full of caribou; then a man in a lumber camp, where you are overtaken by night, tells you that he saw the herd you are after 'way down on the Renous barrens, thirty miles below. You go there, and have the same experience,— signs everywhere, old signs, new signs, but never a caribou. And, ten to one, while you are there, the caribou are sniffing your snowshoe track suspiciously back on the barrens that you have just left.

Even in feeding, when you are hot on their trail and steal forward expecting to see them every moment, it is the same exasperating story. They dig a hole through four feet of packed snow to nibble the reindeer lichen that grows everywhere on the barrens. Before it is half eaten they wander off to the next barren and dig a larger hole; then away to the woods for the gray-green hanging moss that grows on the spruces. Here is a fallen tree half covered with the rich food. Megaleep nibbles a bite or two, then wanders away and away in search of another tree like the one he has just left.

And when you find him at last, the chances are still against you. You are stealing forward cautiously when a fresh sign attracts attention. You stop to examine it a moment. Something gray, dim, misty, seems to drift like a cloud through the trees ahead. You scarcely notice it till, on your right, a stir, and another cloud, and another — The caribou, quick, a score of them! But before your rifle is up and you have found the sights, the gray things melt into the gray woods and drift away; and the stalk begins all over again.

The reason for this restlessness is not far to seek. Megaleep's ancestors followed regular migrations in spring and autumn, like the birds, on the unwooded plains beyond the Arctic Circle. Megaleep never migrates; but the old instinct is in him and will not let him rest. So he wanders through the year, and is never satisfied.

Fortunately nature has been kind to Megaleep in providing him with means to gratify his wandering disposition. In winter, moose and red deer must gather into yards and stay there. With the first heavy storm of December, they gather in small bands here and there on the hardwood ridges, and begin to make paths in the snow, — long, twisted, crooked paths, running for miles in every direction, crossing and recrossing in a tangle utterly hopeless to any head save that of a deer or moose. These paths they keep tramped down and more or less open all winter, so as to feed on the twigs and bark growing on either side. Were it not for this curious provision, a single severe winter would leave hardly a moose or a deer alive in the woods; for their hoofs are sharp and sink deep, and with six feet of snow on a level they can scarcely run half a mile outside their paths without becoming hopelessly stalled or exhausted.

It is this great tangle of paths, by the way, which makes a deer or a moose yard; and not the stupid hole in the snow which is pictured in the geographies and most natural history books.

But Megaleep the Wanderer makes no such provision; he depends upon Mother Nature to take care of him. In summer he is brown, like the great tree trunks among which he moves unseen. Then the frog of his foot expands and grows spongy, so that he can cling to the mountain-side like a goat, or move silently over the dead leaves. In winter he becomes a soft gray, the better to fade into a snowstorm, or to stand concealed in plain sight on the edges of the gray, desolate barrens that he loves. Then the frog of his foot arches up out of the way; the edges of his hoof grow sharp and shell-like, so that he can travel over glare ice without slipping, and cut the crust to dig down for the moss upon which he feeds. The hoofs, moreover, are very large and deeply cleft, so as to spread widely when his weight is on them. When you first find his track in the snow, you rub your eyes, thinking that a huge ox must have passed that way. The dew-claws are also large, and the ankle joint so flexible that it lets them down upon the snow. So Megaleep has a kind of natural snowshoe with which he moves easily over the crust, and, except in very deep, soft snows, wanders at will, while other deer are prisoners in their yards. It is the snapping of these loose hoofs and ankle joints that makes the merry clacking sound as caribou run.

Sometimes, however, they overestimate their abilities, and their wandering disposition brings them into trouble. Once I found a herd of seven up to their backs in soft snow, and tired out,—a strange condition for a caribou to be in. They were taking the affair philosophically, resting till they should gather strength to flounder to some spruce tops where moss was plenty. When I approached gently on snowshoes (I had been hunting them diligently the week before to kill them; but this put a different face on the matter) they gave a bound or two, then settled deep in the snow, and turned their heads and said with their great soft eyes: "You have hunted us. Here we are, at your mercy."

They were very much frightened at first; then I thought they grew a bit curious, as I sat down peaceably in the snow to watch them. One — a doe, more exhausted than the others, and famished — even nibbled a bit of moss that I pushed near her with a stick. I had picked it with gloves, so that the smell of my hand was not on it. After an hour or so, if I moved softly, they let me approach quite up to them without shaking their antlers or renewing their desperate attempts to flounder away. But I did not touch them. That is a degradation which no wild creature will permit when he is free; and I would not take advantage of their helplessness.

Did they starve in the snow? you ask. Oh, no! I went to the place next day and found that they had gained the spruce tops, ploughing through the snow in great bounds, following the track of the strongest, which went ahead to break the way. There they fed and rested, then went to some dense thickets where they passed the night. In a day or two the snow settled and hardened, and they took to their wandering again.

Later, in hunting, I crossed their tracks several times, and once I saw them across a barren; but I left them undisturbed, to follow other trails. We had eaten together; they had fed from my hand; and there is no older truce on earth than that, not even in the unchanging East, where it originated.

Megaleep in a storm is a most curious creature, the nearest thing to a ghost to be found in the woods. More than other animals he feels the falling barometer. His movements at such times drive you to desperation, if you are following him; for he wanders unceasingly. When the storm breaks he has a way of appearing suddenly, as if he were seeking you, when by his trail you thought him miles ahead. And the way he disappears — just melts into the thick driving flakes and the shrouded trees — is most uncanny. Six or seven caribou once played hide-and-seek with me that way, giving me vague glimpses here and there, drawing near to get my scent, yet keeping me looking up wind into the driving snow where I could see nothing distinctly. And all the while they drifted about like so many huge flakes of the storm, watching my every movement, seeing me perfectly.

At such times they fear little, and even lay aside their usual caution. I remember trailing a large herd one day from early morning, keeping near them all the time, and jumping them half a dozen times, yet never getting a glimpse because of their extreme watchfulness. For some reason they were unwilling to leave a small chain of barrens. Perhaps they knew the storm was coming, when they would be safe; and so, instead of swinging off into a ten-mile straightaway trot at the first alarm, they kept dodging back and forth within a two-mile circle. At last, late in the afternoon, I followed the trail to the edge of dense evergreen thickets. Caribou generally rest in open woods or on the windward edge of a barren. Eyes for the open, nose for the cover, is their motto. And I thought, "They know perfectly well I am following them, and so have lain down in that tangle. If I go in, they will hear me; a wood mouse could hardly keep quiet in such a place. If I go round, they will catch my scent; if I wait, so will they; if I jump them, the scrub will cover their retreat perfectly."

As I sat down in the snow to think it over, a heavy rush deep within the thicket told me that something, not I certainly, had again started them. Suddenly the air darkened, and above the excitement of the hunt I felt the storm coming. A storm in the woods is no joke when you are six miles from camp without axe or blanket. I broke away from the trail and started for the head of the second barren on the run. If I could make that, I was safe; for there was a stream near, which led near to camp; and one cannot very well lose a stream, even in a snowstorm. But

Megaleep the Wanderer. 13

before I was halfway the flakes were driving thick and soft in my face. Another half-mile, and one could not see fifty feet in any direction. Still I kept on, holding my course by the wind and my compass. Then, at the foot of the second barren, my snowshoes stumbled into great depressions in the snow, and I found myself on the fresh trail of my caribou again. "If I am lost, I will at least have a caribou steak, and a skin to wrap me up in," I said, and plunged after them. As I went, the old Mother Goose rhyme of nursery days came back and set itself to hunting music:

>Bye, baby bunting,
>Daddy's gone a-hunting,
>For to catch a rabbit skin
>To wrap the baby bunting in.

Presently I began to sing it aloud. It cheered one up in the storm, and the lilt of it kept time to the leaping kind of gallop which is the easiest way to run on snowshoes: "Bye, baby bunting; bye, baby bunting— Hello!"

A dark mass loomed suddenly up before me on the open barren. The storm lightened a bit, before setting in heavier; and there were the caribou just in front of me, standing in a compact mass, the weaker ones in the middle. They had no thought nor fear of me apparently; they showed no sign of anger or uneasiness. Indeed, they barely moved aside as I snowshoed up, in plain sight, without any precaution whatever. And these were the same animals that had fled upon my approach at daylight, and that had escaped me all day with marvelous cunning.

As with other deer, the storm is Megaleep's natural protector. When it comes he thinks that he is safe; that nobody can see him; that the falling snow will fill his tracks and kill his scent; and that whatever follows must speedily seek cover for itself. So he gives up watching, and lies down where he will. So far as his natural enemies are concerned, he is safe in this; for lynx and wolf and panther seek shelter with a falling barometer. They can neither see nor smell; and they are all afraid. I have often noticed that among all animals and birds, from the least to the greatest, there is always a truce when the storms are out.

But the most curious thing I ever stumbled into was a caribou school. That sounds queer; but it is more common in the wilderness than one thinks. All gregarious animals have perfectly well defined social regulations, which the young must learn and respect. To learn them, they go to school in their own interesting way.

Megaleep the Wanderer.

The caribou I am speaking of now are all woodland caribou — larger, finer animals every way than the barren-ground caribou of the desolate unwooded regions farther north. In summer they live singly, rearing their young in deep forest seclusions. There each one does as he pleases. So when you meet a caribou in summer, he is a different creature, and has more unknown and curious ways than when he runs with the herd in midwinter. I remember a solitary old bull that lived on the mountain-side opposite my camp one summer, a most interesting mixture of fear and boldness, of reserve and intense curiosity. After I had hunted him a few times, and he found that my purpose was wholly peaceable, he took to hunting me in the same way, just to find out who I was, and what queer thing I was doing. Sometimes I would see him at sunset on a dizzy cliff across the lake, watching for the curl of smoke or the coming of a canoe. And when I dove in for a swim and went splashing, dog-paddle way, about the island where my tent was, he would walk about in the greatest excitement, and start a dozen times to come down; but always he ran back for another look, as if fascinated. Again he would come down on a burned point near the deep hole where I was fishing, and, hiding his body in the underbrush, would push his horns up into the bare branches of a withered shrub, so as to make them inconspicuous, and stand watching me. As long as he was quiet, it was impossible to see him there; but I could always make him start nervously by flashing a looking-glass, or flopping a fish in the water, or whistling a jolly Irish jig. And when I tied a bright tomato can to a string and set it whirling round my head, or set my handkerchief for a flag on the end of my trout rod, then he could not stand it another minute, but came running down to the shore, to stamp, and fidget, and stare nervously, and scare himself with twenty alarms while trying to make up his mind to swim out and satisfy his burning desire to know all about it. But I am forgetting the caribou schools.

Wherever there are barrens — treeless plains in the midst of dense forest — the caribou collect in small herds as winter comes on, following the old gregarious instinct. Then each one cannot do as he pleases any more; and it is for this winter and spring life together, when laws must be known, and the rights of the individual be laid aside for the good of the herd, that the young are trained.

One afternoon in late summer I was drifting down the Toledi River, casting for trout, when a movement in the bushes ahead caught my attention. A great swampy tract of ground, covered with grass and low brush, spread out on either side the stream. From the canoe I made out two or three waving lines of bushes where some animals were making their way through the swamp towards a strip of big timber which formed a kind of island in the middle.

Pushing my canoe into the grass, I made for a point just astern of the nearest quivering line of bushes. A glance at a bit of soft ground showed me the trail of a mother caribou with her calf. I followed cautiously, the wind being ahead in my favor. They were not hurrying, and I took good pains not to alarm them.

When I reached the timber and crept like a snake through the underbrush, there were the caribou, five or six mother animals, and nearly twice as many little ones, well grown, which had evidently just come in from all directions. They were gathered in a natural opening, fairly clear of bushes, with a fallen tree or two, which served a good purpose later. The sunlight fell across it in great golden bars, making light and shadow to play in; all around was the great marsh, giving protection from enemies; dense underbrush screened them from prying eyes — and this was their schoolroom.

The little ones were pushed out into the middle,

away from the mothers to whom they clung instinctively, and were left to get acquainted with each other, which they did very shyly at first, like so many strange children. It was all new and curious, this meeting of their kind; for till now they had lived in dense solitudes, each one knowing no living creature save its own mother. Some were timid, and backed away as far as possible into the shadow, looking with wild, wide eyes from one to another of the little caribou, and bolting to their mothers' sides at every unusual movement. Others were bold, and took to butting at the first encounter. But careful, kindly eyes watched over them. Now and then a mother caribou would come from the shadows and push a little one gently from his retreat under a bush out into the company. Another would push her way between two heads that lowered at each other threateningly, and say with a warning shake of her head that butting was no good way to get along together. I had once thought, watching a herd on the barrens through my glasses, that they are the gentlest of animals with each other. Here in the little school in the heart of the swamp I found the explanation of things.

For over an hour I lay there and watched, my curiosity growing more eager every moment; for most of what I saw I could not comprehend, having no key, nor understanding why certain youngsters, who needed reproof according to my standards, were let alone, and others kept moving constantly, and still others led aside often to be talked to by their mothers. But at last came a lesson in which all joined, and which could not be misunderstood, not even by a man. It was the jumping lesson.

Caribou are naturally poor jumpers. Beside a deer, who often goes out of his way to jump a fallen tree just for the fun of it, they have no show whatever; though they can travel much farther in a day and much easier. Their gait is a swinging trot, from which it is impossible to jump; and if you frighten them out of their trot into a gallop and keep them at it, they soon grow exhausted. Countless generations on the northern wastes, where there is no need of jumping, have bred this habit, and modified their muscles accordingly. But now a race of caribou has moved south into the woods, where great trees lie fallen across the way, and where, if Megaleep is in a hurry or there is anybody behind him, jumping is a necessity. Still he does n't like it, and avoids it whenever possible. The little ones, left to themselves, would always crawl under a tree, or trot round it. And this is another thing to overcome, and another lesson to be taught in the caribou school.

As I watched them the mothers all came out from the shadows and began trotting round the opening, the little ones keeping close as possible, each one to its mother's side. Then the old ones went faster; the calves were left in a long line stringing out behind. Suddenly the leader veered in to the edge of the timber and went over a fallen tree with a jump; the cows followed splendidly, rising on one side, falling gracefully on the other, like gray waves racing past the end of a jetty. But the first little one dropped his head obstinately at the tree and stopped short. The next one did the same thing; only he ran his head into the first one's legs and knocked them out from under him. The others whirled with a *ba-a-a-ah*, and scampered round the tree and up to their mothers, who had turned now and stood watching anxiously to see the effect of their lesson. Then it began over again.

It was true kindergarten teaching; for under guise of a frolic the calves were being taught a needful lesson,— not only to jump, but, far more important than that, to follow a leader, and to go where he goes without question or hesitation. For the leaders on the barrens are wise old bulls that make no mistakes. Most of the little caribou took to the sport very well,

Megaleep the Wanderer.

and presently followed the mothers over the low hurdles. But a few were timid; and then came the most intensely interesting bit of the whole strange school, when a little one would be led to a tree and butted from behind till he took the jump.

There was no "consent of the governed" in that governing. The mother knew, and the calf did n't, just what was good for him.

It was this last lesson that broke up the school. Just in front of my hiding place a tree fell out into the opening. A mother caribou brought her calf up to this unsuspectingly, and leaped over, expecting the little one to follow. As she struck she whirled like a top and stood like a beautiful statue, her head pointing in my direction. Her eyes were bright with fear, the ears set forward, the nostrils spread to catch every tainted atom from the air. Then she turned and glided silently away, the little one close to her side, looking up and touching her frequently as if to whisper, *What is it? what is it?* but making no sound. There was no signal given, no alarm of any kind that I could understand; yet the lesson stopped instantly. The caribou glided away like shadows. Over across the opening a bush swayed here and there; a leaf quivered as if something touched its branch. Then the schoolroom was empty and the woods all still.

There is another curious habit of Megaleep; and this one I am utterly at a loss to account for. When he is old and feeble, and the tireless muscles will no longer carry him with the herd over the wind-swept barrens, and he falls sick at last, he goes to a spot far away in the woods, where generations of his ancestors have preceded him, and there lays him down to die. It is the caribou burying ground; and all the animals of a certain district, or a certain herd (I am unable to tell which), will go there when sick or sore wounded, if they have strength enough to reach the spot. For it is far away from the scene of their summer homes and their winter wanderings.

I know one such place, and visited it twice from my summer camp. It is in a dark tamarack swamp by a lonely lake at the head of the Little-South-West Miramichi River, in New Brunswick. I found it one summer when trying to force my way from the big lake to a smaller one, where trout were plenty. In the midst of the swamp I stumbled upon a pair of caribou skeletons, which surprised me; for there were no hunters within a hundred miles, and at that time the lake had lain for many years unvisited. I thought of fights between bucks, and bull moose, how two bulls will sometimes lock horns in a rush, and are too weakened to break the lock, and so die together of exhaustion. Caribou are more peaceable; they rarely fight that way; and, besides, the horns here were not locked together, but lying well apart. As I searched about, looking for the explanation of things, thinking of wolves, yet wondering why the bones were not gnawed, I found another skeleton, much older, then four or five more; some quite fresh, others crumbling into mould. Bits of old bone and some splendid antlers were scattered here and there through the underbrush; and when I scraped away the dead leaves and moss, there were older bones and fragments mouldering beneath.

I scarcely understood the meaning of it at the time; but since then I have met men, Indians and hunters, who have spent much time in the wilderness, who speak of "bone yards" which they have discovered, places where they can go at any time and be sure of finding a good set of caribou antlers. And they say that the caribou go there to die.

All animals, when feeble with age, or sickly, or wounded, have the habit of going away deep into the loneliest coverts, and there lying down where the leaves shall presently cover them. So that one rarely finds a dead bird or animal in the woods where thousands die yearly. Even your dog, that was born and lived by your house, often disappears when you thought him too feeble to walk. Death calls him gently; the old wolf stirs deep within him, and he goes away where the master he served will never find him. And so with your cat, which is only skin-deep a domestic animal; and so with your canary, which in death alone would be free, and beats his failing wings against the cage in which he lived so long content. But these all go away singly, each to his own place. The caribou is the only animal I know that remembers, when his separation comes, the ties which bound him to the herd winter after winter, through sun and storm, in the forest where all was peace and plenty, and on the lonely barrens where the gray wolf howled on his track; so that he turns with his last strength from the herd he is leaving to the greater herd which has gone before him — still following his leaders, remembering his first lesson to the end.

Sometimes I have wondered whether this also were taught in the caribou school; whether once in his life Megaleep were led to the spot and made to pass through it, so that he should feel its meaning and remember. That is not likely; for the one thing which an animal cannot understand is death. And there were no signs of living caribou anywhere near the place that I discovered; though down at the other end of the lake their tracks were everywhere.

There are other questions, which one can only ask without answering. Is this silent gathering merely a tribute to the old law of the herd, or does Megaleep, with his last strength, still think to cheat his old enemy, and go away where the wolf that followed him all his life shall not find him? How was his resting place first selected, and what leaders searched out the ground? What sound or sign, what murmur of wind in the pines, or lap of ripples on the shore, or song of the veery at twilight made them pause and say, *Here is the place?* How does he know, he whose thoughts are all of life, and who never looked on death, where the great silent herd is that no caribou ever sees but once? And what strange instinct guides Megaleep to the spot where all his wanderings end at last?

II. KILLOOLEET, LITTLE SWEET-VOICE.

THE day was cold, the woods were wet, and the weather was beastly altogether when Killooleet first came and sang on my ridgepole. The fishing was poor down in the big lake, and there were signs of civilization here and there, in the shape of settlers' cabins, which we did not like; so we had pushed up river, Simmo and I, thirty miles in the rain, to a favorite camping ground on a smaller lake, where we had the wilderness all to ourselves.

The rain was still falling, and the lake whitecapped, and the forest all misty and wind-blown when we ran our canoes ashore by the old cedar that marked our landing place. First we built a big fire to dry some boughs to sleep upon; then we built our houses, Simmo a bark *commoosie*, and I a little tent; and I was inside, getting dry clothes out of a rubber bag, when I heard a white-throated sparrow calling cheerily his Indian name, *O hear, sweet Killooleet-lillooleet-lillooleet!* And the sound was so sunny, so good to hear in the steady drip of rain on the roof, that I went out to see the little fellow who had bid us welcome to the wilderness.

Simmo had heard too. He was on his hands and knees, just his dark face peering by the corner stake of his *commoosie*, so as to see better the little singer on my tent. — " Have better weather and better luck now. Killooleet sing on ridgepole," he said confidently. Then we spread some cracker crumbs for the guest and turned in to sleep till better times.

That was the beginning of a long acquaintance. It was also the first of many social calls from a whole colony of white-throats (Tom-Peabody birds) that lived on the mountain-side just behind my tent, and that came one by one to sing to us, and to get acquainted, and to share our crumbs. Sometimes, too, in rainy weather, when the woods seemed wetter than the lake, and Simmo would be sleeping philosophically, and I reading, or tying trout flies in the tent, I would hear a gentle stir and a rustle or two just outside, under the tent fly. Then, if I crept out quietly, I would find Killooleet exploring my goods to find where the crackers grew, or just resting contentedly under the fly where it was dry and comfortable.

It was good to live there among them, with the mountain at our backs and the lake at our feet, and peace breathing in every breeze or brooding silently over the place at twilight. Rain or shine, day or night, these white-throated sparrows are the sunniest, cheeriest folk to be found anywhere in the woods. I grew to understand and love the Milicete name, Killooleet, Little Sweet-Voice, for its expressiveness. "Hour-Bird" the Micmacs call him; for they say he sings every hour, and so tells the time, "all same's one white man's watch." And indeed there is rarely an hour, day or night, in the northern woods when you cannot hear Killooleet singing. Other birds grow silent after they have won their mates, or they grow fat and lazy as summer advances, or absorbed in the care of their young, and have no time nor thought for singing. But not so Killooleet. He is kinder to his mate after he has won her, and never lets selfishness or the summer steal away his music; for he knows that the woods are brighter for his singing.

Sometimes, at night, I would take a brand from the fire, and follow a deer path that wound about the mountain, or steal away into a dark thicket and strike a parlor match. As the flame shot up, lighting its little circle of waiting leaves, there would be a stir beside me in the underbrush, or overhead in the fir; then tinkling out of the darkness, like a brook under the snow, would come the low clear strain of melody that always set my heart a-dancing, — *I'm here, sweet Killooleet-lillooleet-lillooleet*, the good-night song of my gentle neighbor. Then along the path a little way, and another match, and another song to make one better and his rest sweeter.

By day I used to listen to them, hours long at a stretch, practicing to perfect their song. These were the younger birds, of course; and for a long time they puzzled me. Those who know Killooleet's song will remember that it begins with three clear sweet notes; but very few have observed the break between the second and third of these. I noticed, first of all, that certain birds would start the song twenty times in succession, yet never get beyond the second note. And when I crept up, to find out about it, I would find them sitting disconsolately, deep in shadow, instead of out in the light where they love to sing, with a pitiful little droop of wings and tail, and the air of failure and dejection in every movement. Then again these same singers would touch the third note, and always in such cases they would prolong the last trill, the *lillooleet-lillooleet* (the *Peabody-Peabody*, as some think of it), to an indefinite length, instead of stopping at the second or third repetition, which is the rule with good singers. Then they would come out of the shadow, and stir about briskly, and sing again with an air of triumph.

One day, while lying still in the underbrush watching a wood mouse, Killooleet, a fine male bird and a perfect singer, came and sang on a branch just over my head, not noticing me. Then I discovered that there is a trill, a tiny grace note or yodel, at the end of his second note. I listened carefully to other singers, as close as I could get, and found that it is always there, and is the one difficult part of the song. You must be very close to the bird to appreciate the beauty of this little yodel; for ten feet away it sounds like a faint cluck interrupting the flow of the third note; and a little farther away you cannot hear it at all.

Whatever its object, Killooleet regards this as the indispensable part of his song, and never goes on to the third note unless he gets the second perfectly. That accounts for the many times when one hears only the first two notes. That accounts also for the occasional prolonged trill which one hears; for when a young bird has tried many times for his grace note without success, and then gets it unexpectedly, he is

He had mastered the trill perfectly

so pleased with himself that he forgets he is not Whippoorwill, who tries to sing as long as the brook without stopping, and so keeps up the final *lillooleet-lillooleet* as long as he has an atom of breath left to do it with.

But of all the Killooleets, — and there were many that I soon recognized, either by their songs, or by some peculiarity in their striped caps or brown jackets, — the most interesting was the one who first perched on my ridgepole and bade me welcome to his camping ground. I soon learned to distinguish him easily; his cap was very bright, and his white cravat very full, and his song never stopped at the second note, for he had mastered the trill perfectly. Then, too, he was more friendly and fearless than all the others. The morning after our arrival (it was better weather, as Simmo and Killooleet had predicted) we were eating breakfast by the fire, when he lit on the ground close by, and turned his head sidewise to look at us curiously. I tossed him a big crumb, which made him run away in fright; but when he thought we were not looking he stole back, touched, tasted, ate the whole of it. And when I threw him another crumb, he hopped to meet it.

After that he came regularly to meals, and would look critically over the tin plate which I placed at my feet, and pick and choose daintily from the cracker and trout and bacon and porridge which I offered him. Soon he began to take bits away with him, and I could hear him, just inside the fringe of underbrush, persuading his mate to come too and share his plate. But she was much shyer than he; it was several days before I noticed her flitting in and out of the shadowy underbrush; and when I tossed her the first crumb, she flew away in a terrible fright. Gradually, however, Killooleet persuaded her that we were kindly, and she came often to meals; but she would never come near, to eat from my tin plate, till after I had gone away.

Never a day now passed that one or both of the birds did not rest on my tent. When I put my head out, like a turtle out of his shell, in the early morning to look at the weather, Killooleet would look down from the projecting end of the ridgepole and sing good-morning. And when I had been out late on the lake, night-fishing, or following the inlet for beaver, or watching the grassy points for caribou, or just drifting along shore silently to catch the night sounds and smells of the woods, I would listen with childish anticipation for Killooleet's welcome as I approached the landing. He had learned to recognize the sounds of my coming, the rub of a careless paddle, the ripple of water under the bow, or the grating of pebbles on the beach; and with Simmo asleep, and the fire low, it was good to be welcomed back by a cheery little voice in the darkness; for he always sang when he heard me. Sometimes I would try to surprise him; but his sleep was too light and his ears too keen. The canoe would glide up to the old cedar and touch the shore noiselessly; but with the first crunch of gravel under my foot, or the rub of my canoe as I lifted it out, he would waken; and his song, all sweetness and cheer, *I'm here, sweet Killooleet-lillooleet-lillooleet*, would ripple out of the dark underbrush where his nest was.

I am glad now to think that I never saw that nest, though it was scarcely ten yards from my tent, until after the young had flown, and Killooleet cared no more about it. I knew the bush in which it was, close by the deer path; could pick out from my fireplace the thick branch that sheltered it; for I often watched the birds coming and going. I have no doubt that Killooleet would have welcomed me there without fear; but his mate never laid aside her shyness about it, never went to it directly when I was looking, and I knew he would like me better if I respected her little secret.

Soon, from the mate's infrequent visits, and from

the amount of food which Killooleet took away with him, I knew she was brooding her eggs. And when at last both birds came together, and, instead of helping themselves hungrily, each took the largest morsel he could carry and hurried away to the nest, I knew that the little ones were come; and I spread the plate more liberally, and moved it away to the foot of the old cedar, where Killooleet's mate would not be afraid to come at any time.

One day, not long after, as I sat at a late breakfast after the morning's fishing, there was a great stir in the underbrush. Presently Killooleet came skipping out, all fuss and feathers, running back and forth with an air of immense importance between the last bush and the plate by the cedar, crying out in his own way, "Here it is, here it is, all right, just by the old tree as usual. Crackers, trout, brown bread, porridge; come on, come on; don't be afraid. *He's* here, but he won't harm. I know him. Come on, come on!"

Soon his little gray mate appeared under the last bush, and after much circumspection came hopping towards the breakfast; and after her, in a long line, five little Killooleets, hopping, fluttering, cheeping, stumbling, — all in a fright at the big world, but all in a desperate hurry for crackers and porridge *ad libitum;* now casting hungry eyes at the plate under the old cedar, now stopping to turn their heads sidewise to see the big kind animal with only two legs, that Killooleet had told them about, no doubt, many times.

After that we had often seven guests to breakfast, instead of two. It was good to hear them, the lively *tink, tink-a-tink* of their little bills on the tin plate in a merry tattoo, as I ate my own tea and trout thankfully. I had only to raise my eyes to see them in a bobbing brown ring about my bounty; and, just beyond them, the lap of ripples on the beach, the lake glinting far away in the sunshine, and a bark canoe fretting at the landing, swinging, veering, nodding at the ripples, and beckoning me to come away as soon as I had finished my breakfast.

Before the little Killooleets had grown accustomed to things, however, occurred the most delicious bit of our summer camping. It was only a day or two after their first appearance; they knew simply that crumbs and a welcome awaited them at my camp, but had not yet learned that the tin plate in the cedar roots was their special portion. Simmo had gone off at daylight, looking up beaver signs for his fall trapping. I had just returned from the morning fishing, and was getting breakfast, when I saw an otter come out into the lake from a cold brook over on the east shore.

Grabbing a handful of figs, and some pilot bread from the cracker box, I paddled away after the otter; for that is an animal which one has small chance to watch nowadays. Besides, I had found a den over near the brook, and I wanted to find out, if possible, how a mother otter teaches her young to swim. For, though otters live much in the water and love it, the young ones are afraid of it as so many kittens. So the mother —

But I must tell about that elsewhere. I did not find out that day; for the young were already good swimmers. I watched the den two or three hours from a good hiding place, and got several glimpses of the mother and the little ones. On the way back I ran into a little bay where a mother shelldrake was teaching her brood to dive and catch trout. There was also a big frog there that always sat in the same place, and that I used to watch. Then I thought of a trap, two miles away, which Simmo had set, and went to see if Nemox, the cunning fisher, who destroys the sable traps in winter, had been caught at his own game. So it was afternoon, and I was hungry, when I paddled back to camp. It occurred to me suddenly that Killooleet might be hungry too; for I had neglected to feed him. He had grown sleek and comfortable of late, and never went insect hunting when he could get cold fried trout and corn bread.

I landed silently and stole up to the tent to see if he were exploring under the fly, as he sometimes did when I was away. A curious sound, a hollow *tunk, tunk, tunk, tunk-a-tunk*, grew louder as I approached. I stole to the big cedar, where I could see the fireplace and the little opening before my tent, and noticed first that I had left the cracker box open (it was almost empty) when I hurried away after the otter. The curious sound was inside, growing more eager every moment — *tunk, tunk, tunk-a-trrrrrrr-runk, tunk, tunk!*

I crept on my hands and knees to the box, to see what queer thing had found his way to the crackers, and peeped cautiously over the edge. There were Killooleet, and Mrs. Killooleet, and the five little Killooleets, just seven hopping brown backs and bobbing heads, helping themselves to the crackers. And the sound of their bills on the empty box made the jolliest tattoo that ever came out of a camping kit.

I crept away more cautiously than I had come, and, standing carelessly in my tent door, whistled the call I always used in feeding the birds. Like a flash Killooleet appeared on the edge of the cracker box, looking very much surprised. "I thought you were away; why, I thought you were away," he seemed to be saying. Then he clucked, and the *tunk-a-tunk* ceased instantly. Another cluck, and Mrs. Killooleet appeared, looking frightened; then, one after another, the five little Killooleets bobbed up; and there they sat in a solemn row on the edge of the cracker box, turning their heads sidewise to see me better.

"There!" said Killooleet, "did n't I tell you he would n't hurt you?" And like five winks the five little Killooleets were back in the box, and the *tunk-a-tunking* began again.

This assurance that they might do as they pleased, and help themselves undisturbed to whatever they found, seemed to remove the last doubt from the mind of even the little gray mate. After that they stayed most of the time close about my tent, and were never so far away, or so busy insect hunting, that they would not come when I whistled and scattered crumbs. The little Killooleets grew amazingly, and no wonder! They were always eating, always hungry. I took good pains to give them less than they wanted, and so had the satisfaction of feeding them often, and of finding their tin plate picked clean whenever I came back from fishing.

Killooleet, Little Sweet-Voice.

Did the woods seem lonely to Killooleet when we paddled away at last and left the wilderness for another year? That is a question which I would give much, or watch long, to answer. There is always a regret at leaving a good camping ground, but I had never packed up so unwillingly before. Killooleet was singing, cheery as ever; but my own heart gave a minor chord of sadness to his trill that was not there when he sang on my ridgepole. Before leaving I had baked a loaf, big and hard, which I fastened with stakes at the foot of the old cedar, with a tin plate under it and a bark roof above, so that when it rained, and insects were hidden under the leaves, and their hunting was no fun because the woods were wet, Killooleet and his little ones would find food, and remember me. And so we paddled away and left him to the wilderness.

A year later my canoe touched the same old landing. For ten months I had been in the city, where Killooleet never sings, and where the wilderness is only a memory. In the fall, on some long tramps, I had occasional glimpses of the little singer, solitary now and silent, stealing southward ahead of the winter. And in the spring he showed himself rarely in the underbrush on country roads, eager, restless, chirping, hurrying northward where the streams were clear and the big woods budding. But never a song in all that time; my ears were hungry for his voice as I leaped out to run eagerly to the big cedar. There were the stakes, and the tin plate, and the bark roof all crushed by the snows of winter. The bread was gone; what Killooleet had spared, Tookhees the wood mouse had eaten thankfully. I found the old tent poles and put up my house leisurely, a hundred happy memories thronging about me. In the midst of them came a call, a clear whistle, — and there he was, the same full cravat, the same bright cap, and the same perfect song to set my nerves a-tingling: *I'm here, sweet Killooleet-lillooleet-lillooleet!* And when I put crumbs by the old fireplace, he flew down to help himself, and went off with the biggest one, as of yore, to his nest by the deer path.

III. KAGAX THE BLOODTHIRSTY.

HIS is the story of one day, the last one, in the life of Kagax the Weasel, who turns white in winter, and yellow in spring, and brown in summer, the better to hide his villainy.

It was early twilight when Kagax came out of his den in the rocks, under the old pine that lightning had blasted. Day and night were meeting swiftly but warily, as they always meet in the woods. The life of the sunshine came stealing nestwards and denwards in the peace of a long day and a full stomach; the night life began to stir in its coverts, eager, hungry, whining. Deep in the wild raspberry thickets a wood thrush rang his vesper bell softly; from the mountain top a night hawk screamed back an answer, and came booming down to earth, where the insects were rising in myriads. Near the thrush a striped chipmunk sat chunk-a-chunking his sleepy curiosity at a burned log which a bear had just torn open for red ants; while down on the lake shore a cautious *plash-plash* told where a cow moose had come out of the alders with her calf to sup on the yellow lily roots and sip the freshest water. Everywhere life was stirring; everywhere cries, calls, squeaks, chirps, rustlings, which only the wood-dweller knows how to interpret, broke in upon the twilight stillness.

Kagax grinned and showed all his wicked little teeth as the many voices went up from lake and stream and forest. "Mine, all mine — to kill," he snarled, and his eyes began to glow deep red. Then he stretched one sinewy paw after another, rolled over, climbed a tree, and jumped down from a swaying twig to get the sleep all out of him.

Kagax had slept too much, and was mad with the world. The night before, he had killed from sunset to sunrise, and much tasting of blood had made him heavy. So he had slept all day long, only stirring once to kill a partridge that had drummed near his den and waked him out of sleep. But he was too heavy to hunt then, so he crept back again, leaving the bird untasted under the end of his own drumming log. Now Kagax was eager to make up for lost time; for all time is lost to Kagax that is not spent in killing. That is why he runs night and day, and barely tastes the blood of his victims, and sleeps only an hour or two of cat naps at a time — just long enough to gather energy for more evil doing.

As he stretched himself again, a sudden barking and snickering came from a giant spruce on the hill just above. Meeko, the red squirrel, had discovered a new jay's nest, and was making a sensation over it, as he does over everything that he has not happened to see before. Had he known who was listening, he would have risked his neck in a headlong rush for safety; for all the wild things fear Kagax as they fear death. But no wild thing ever knows till too late that a weasel is near.

Kagax listened a moment, a ferocious grin on his pointed face; then he stole towards the sound. "I intended to kill those young hares first," he thought, "but this fool squirrel will stretch my legs better, and point my nose, and get the sleep out of me — There he is, in the big spruce!"

Kagax had not seen the squirrel; but that did not matter; he can locate a victim better with his nose or ears than he can with his eyes. The moment he was sure of the place, he rushed forward without caution. Meeko was in the midst of a prolonged snicker at the scolding jays, when he heard a scratch on the bark below, turned, looked down, and fled with a cry of terror. Kagax was already halfway up the tree, the red fire blazing in his eyes.

The squirrel rushed to the end of a branch, jumped to a smaller spruce, ran that up to the top; then, because his fright had made him forget the tree paths that ordinarily he knew very well, he sprang out and down to the ground, a clear fifty feet, breaking his fall by catching and holding for an instant a swaying fir tip on the way. Then he rushed pell-mell over logs and rocks, and through the underbrush to a maple, and from that across a dozen trees to another giant spruce, where he ran up and down desperately over half the branches, crossing and crisscrossing his trail, and dropped panting at last into a little crevice under a broken limb. There he crouched into the smallest possible space and watched, with an awful fear in his eyes, the rough trunk below.

Far behind him came Kagax, grim, relentless, silent as death. He paid no attention to scratching claws nor swaying branches, never looking for the jerking red tip of Meeko's tail, nor listening for the loud thump of his feet when he struck the ground. A pair of brave little flycatchers saw the chase and rushed at the common enemy, striking him with their beaks, and raising an outcry that brought a score of frightened, clamoring birds to the scene.

Kagax the Bloodthirsty.

But Kagax never heeded. His whole being seemed to be concentrated in the point of his nose. He followed like a bloodhound to the top of the second spruce, sniffed here and there till he caught the scent of Meeko's passage through the air, ran to the end of a branch in the same direction and leaped to the ground, landing not ten feet from the spot where the squirrel had struck a moment before. There he picked up the trail, followed over logs and rocks to the maple, up to the third branch, and across fifty yards of intervening branches to the giant spruce where his victim sat half paralyzed, watching from his crevice.

Here Kagax was more deliberate. Left and right, up and down he went with deadly patience, from the lowest branch to the top, a hundred feet above, following every cross and winding of the trail. A dozen times he stopped, went back, picked up the fresher trail, and went on again. A dozen times he passed within a few feet of his victim, smelling him strongly, but scorning to use his eyes till his nose had done its perfect work. So he came to the last turn, followed the last branch, his nose to the bark, straight to the crevice under the broken branch, where Meeko crouched shivering, knowing it was all over.

There was a cry, that no one heeded in the woods;

there was a flash of sharp teeth, and the squirrel fell, striking the ground with a heavy thump. Kagax ran down the trunk, sniffed an instant at the body without touching it, and darted away to the form among the ferns. He had passed it at daylight when he was too heavy for killing.

Halfway to the lake, he stopped; a thrilling song from a dead spruce top bubbled out over the darkening woods. When a hermit thrush sings like that, his nest is somewhere just below. Kagax began twisting in and out like a snake among the bushes, till a stir in a tangle of raspberry vines, which no ears but his or an owl's would ever notice, made him shrink close to the ground and look up. The red fire blazed in his eyes again; for there was Mother Thrush just settling onto her nest, not five feet from his head.

To climb the raspberry vines without shaking them, and so alarming the bird, was out of the question; but there was a fire-blasted tree just behind. Kagax climbed it stealthily on the side away from the bird, crept to a branch over the nest, and leaped down. Mother Thrush was preening herself sleepily, feeling the grateful warmth of her eggs and listening to the wonderful song overhead, when the blow came. Before she knew what it was, the sharp teeth had met

Kagax the Bloodthirsty. 47

in her brain. The pretty nest would never again wait for a brooding mother in the twilight.

All the while the wonderful song went on; for the hermit thrush, pouring his soul out, far above on the dead spruce top, heard not a sound of the tragedy below.

Kagax flung the warm body aside savagely, bit through the ends of the three eggs, wishing they were young thrushes, and leaped to the ground. There he just tasted the brain of his victim to whet his appetite, listened a moment, crouching among the dead leaves, to the melody overhead, wishing it were darker, so that the hermit would come down and he could end his wicked work. Then he glided away to the young hares.

There were five of them in the form, hidden among the coarse brakes of a little opening. Kagax went straight to the spot. A weasel never forgets. He killed them all, one after another, slowly, deliberately, by a single bite through the spine, tasting only the blood of the last one. Then he wriggled down among the warm bodies and waited, his nose to the path by which Mother Hare had gone away. He knew well she would soon be coming back.

Presently he heard her, *put-a-put, put-a-put*, hopping along the path, with a waving line of ferns to show just where she was. Kagax wriggled lower among his helpless victims; his eyes blazed red again, so red that Mother Hare saw them and stopped short. Then Kagax sat up straight among the dead babies and screeched in her face.

The poor creature never moved a step; she only crouched low before her own door and began to shiver violently. Kagax ran up to her; raised himself on his hind legs so as to place his fore paws on her neck; chose his favorite spot behind the ears, and bit. The hare straightened out, the quivering ceased. A tiny drop of blood followed the sharp teeth on either side. Kagax licked it greedily and hurried away, afraid to spoil his hunt by drinking.

But he had scarcely entered the woods, running heedlessly, when the moss by a great stone stirred with a swift motion. There was a squeak of fright as Kagax jumped forward like lightning — but too late. Tookhees, the timid little wood mouse, who was digging under the moss for twin-flower roots to feed his little ones, had heard the enemy coming, and dove headlong into his hole, just in time to escape the snap of Kagax's teeth.

That angered the fiery little weasel like poking a stick at him. To be caught napping, or to be heard running through the woods, is more than he can pos-

Kagax the Bloodthirsty. 49

sibly stand. His eyes fairly snapped as he began digging furiously. Below, he could hear a chorus of faint squeaks, the clamor of young wood mice for their supper. But a few inches down, and the hole doubled under a round stone, then vanished between two roots close together. Try as he would, Kagax could only wear his claws out, without making any progress. He tried to force his shoulders through; for a weasel thinks he can go anywhere. But the hole was too small. Kagax cried out in rage and took up the trail. A dozen times he ran it from the hole to the torn moss, where Tookhees had been digging roots, and back again; then, sure that all the wood mice were inside, he tried to tear his way between the obstinate roots. As well try to claw down the tree itself.

All the while Tookhees, who always has just such a turn in his tunnel, and who knows perfectly when he is safe, crouched just below the roots, looking up with steady little eyes, like two black beads, at his savage pursuer, and listening in a kind of dumb terror to his snarls of rage.

Kagax gave it up at last and took to running in circles. Wider and wider he went, running swift and silent, his nose to the ground, seeking other mice on whom to wreak his vengeance. Suddenly he struck a fresh trail and ran it straight to the clearing where a foolish field mouse had built a nest in a tangle of dry brakes. Kagax caught and killed the mother as she rushed out in alarm. Then he tore the nest open and killed all the little ones. He tasted the blood of one and went on again.

The failure to catch the wood mouse still rankled in his head and kept his eyes bright red. Suddenly he turned from his course along the lake shore; he began to climb the ridge. Up and up he went, crossing a dozen trails that ordinarily he would have followed, till he came to where a dead tree had fallen and lodged against a big spruce, near the summit. There he crouched in the underbrush and waited.

Up near the top of the dead tree, a pair of pine martens had made their den in the hollow trunk, and reared a family of young martens that drew Kagax's evil thoughts like a magnet. The marten belongs to the weasel's own family; therefore, as a choice bit of revenge, Kagax would rather kill him than anything else. A score of times he had crouched in this same place and waited for his chance. But the marten is larger and stronger every way than the weasel, and, though shyer, almost as savage in a fight. And Kagax was afraid.

But to-night Kagax was in a more vicious mood than ever before; and a weasel's temper is always the most vicious thing in the woods. He stole forward at last and put his nose to the foot of the leaning tree. Two fresh trails went out; none came back. Kagax followed them far enough to be sure that both martens were away hunting; then he turned and ran like a flash up the incline and into the den.

In a moment he came out, licking his chops greedily. Inside, the young martens lay just as they had been left by the mother; only they began to grow very cold. Kagax ran to the great spruce, along a branch into another tree; then to the ground by a dizzy jump. There he ran swiftly for a good half hour in a long diagonal down towards the lake, crisscrossing his trail here and there as he ran.

Once more his night's hunting began, with greater zeal than before. He was hungry now; his nose grew keen as a brier for every trail. A faint smell stopped him, so faint that the keenest-nosed dog or fox would have passed without turning, the smell of a brooding partridge on her eggs. There she was, among the roots of a pine, sitting close and blending perfectly with the roots and the brown needles. Kagax moved like a shadow; his nose found the bird; before she could spring he was on her back, and his teeth had done their evil work. Once more he tasted the fresh brains with keen relish. He broke all the eggs, so that none else might profit by his hunting, and went on again.

On some moist ground, under a hemlock, he came upon the fresh trail of a wandering hare — no simple, unsuspecting mother, coming back to her babies, but a big, strong, suspicious fellow, who knew how to make a run for his life. Kagax was still fresh and eager; here was game that would stretch his muscles. The red lust of killing flamed into his eyes as he jumped away on the trail.

Soon, by the long distances between tracks, he knew that the hare was startled. The scent was fresher now, so fresh that he could follow it in the air, without putting his nose to the ground.

Suddenly a great commotion sounded among the bushes just ahead, where a moment before all was still. The hare had been lying there, watching his back track to see what was following. When he saw the red eyes of Kagax, he darted away wildly. A few hundred yards, and the foolish hare, who could run far faster than his pursuer, dropped in the bushes again to watch and see if the weasel was still after him.

Kagax was following, swiftly, silently. Again the hare bounded away, only to stop and scare himself into fits by watching his own trail till the red eyes of the weasel blazed into view. So it went on for a half hour, through brush and brake and swamp, till the hare had lost all his wits and began to run wildly in small circles. Then Kagax turned, ran the back track a little way, and crouched flat on the ground.

In a moment the hare came tearing along on his own trail — straight towards the yellow-brown ball under a fern tip. Kagax waited till he was almost run over; then he sprang up and screeched. That ended the chase. The hare just dropped on his fore paws. Kagax jumped for his head; his teeth met; the hunger began to gnaw, and he drank his fill greedily.

For a time the madness of the chase seemed to be in the blood he drank. Keener than ever to kill, he darted away on a fresh trail. But soon his feast began to tell; his feet grew heavy. Angry at himself, he lay down to sleep their weight away.

Far behind him, under the pine by the partridge's nest, a long dark shadow seemed to glide over the ground. A pointed nose touched the leaves here and there; over the nose a pair of fierce little eyes glowed deep red as Kagax's own. So the shadow came to the partridge's nest, passed over it, minding not the scent of broken eggs nor of the dead bird, but only the scent of the weasel, and vanished into the underbrush on the trail.

Kagax woke with a start and ran on. A big bullfrog croaked down on the shore. Kagax stalked and killed him, leaving his carcass untouched among the lily pads. A dead pine in a thicket attracted his suspicion. He climbed it swiftly, found a fresh round hole, and tumbled in upon a mother bird and a family of young woodpeckers. He killed them all, tasting the brains again, and hunted the tree over for the father bird, the great black logcock that makes the wilderness ring with his tattoo. But the logcock heard claws on the bark and flew to another tree, making a great commotion in the darkness as he blundered along, but not knowing what it was that had startled him.

So the night wore on, with Kagax killing in every thicket, yet never satisfied with killing. He thought longingly of the hard winter, when game was scarce, and he had made his way out over the snow to the settlement, and lived among the chicken coops. "Twenty big hens in one roost — that was killing," snarled Kagax savagely, as he strangled two young herons in their nest, while the mother bird went on with her frogging, not ten yards away among the lily pads, and never heard a rustle.

Kagax the Bloodthirsty.

Toward morning he turned homeward, making his way back in a circle along the top of the ridge where his den was, and killing as he went. He had tasted too much; his feet grew heavier than they had ever been before. He thought angrily that he would have to sleep another whole day. And to sleep a whole day, while the wilderness was just beginning to swarm with life, filled Kagax with snarling rage.

A mother hare darted away from her form as the weasel's wicked eyes looked in upon her. Kagax killed the little ones and had started after the mother, when a shiver passed over him and he turned back to listen. He had been moving more slowly of late; several times he had looked behind him with the feeling that he was followed. He stole back to the hare's form and lay hidden, watching his back track. He shivered again. "If it were not stronger than I, it would not follow my trail," thought Kagax. The fear of a hunted thing came upon him. He remembered the marten's den, the strangled young ones, the two trails that left the leaning tree. "They must have turned back long ago," thought Kagax, and darted away. His back was cold now, cold as ice.

But his feet grew very heavy ere he reached his den. A faint light began to show over the mountain across the lake. Killooleet, the white-throated sparrow, saw it, and his clear morning song tinkled out of the dark underbrush. Kagax's eyes glowed red again; he stole toward the sound for a last kill. Young sparrows' brains are a dainty dish; he would eat his fill, since he must sleep all day. He found the nest; he had placed his fore paws against the tree that held it, when he dropped suddenly; the shivers began to course all over him. Just below, from a stub in a dark thicket, a deep *Whooo-hoo-hoo!* rolled out over the startled woods.

It was Kookooskoos, the great horned owl, who generally hunts only in the evening twilight, but who, with growing young ones to feed, sometimes uses the morning twilight as well. Kagax lay still as a stone. Over him the sparrows, knowing the danger, crouched low in their nest, not daring to move a claw lest the owl should hear.

Behind him the same shadow that had passed over the partridge's nest looked into the hare's form with fierce red eyes. It followed Kagax's trail over that of the mother hare, turned back, sniffed the earth, and came hurrying silently along the ridge.

Kagax crept stealthily out of the thicket. He had an awful fear now of his feet; for, heavy with the blood he had eaten, they would rustle the leaves, or scratch on the stones, that all night long they had

Two sets of strong curved claws dropped down from the shadow

Kagax the Bloodthirsty. 57

glided over in silence. He was near his den now. He could see the old pine that lightning had blasted, towering against the sky over the dark spruces.

Again the deep *Whooo-hoo-hoo!* rolled over the hillside. To Kagax, who gloats over his killing except when he is afraid, it became an awful accusation. "Who has killed where he cannot eat? who strangled a brooding bird? who murdered his own kin?" came thundering through the woods. Kagax darted for his den. His hind feet struck a rotten twig that they should have cleared; it broke with a sharp snap. In an instant a huge shadow swept down from the stub and hovered over the sound. Two fierce yellow eyes looked in upon Kagax, crouching and trying to hide under a fir tip.

Kagax whirled when the eyes found him and two sets of strong curved claws dropped down from the shadow. With a savage snarl he sprang up, and his teeth met; but no blood followed the bite, only a flutter of soft brown feathers. Then one set of sharp claws gripped his head; another set met deep in his back. Kagax was jerked swiftly into the air, and his evil doing was ended forever.

There was a faint rustle in the thicket as the shadow of Kookooskoos swept away to his nest. The long lithe form of a pine marten glided straight to the fir tip, where Kagax had been a moment before. His movements were quick, nervous, silent; his eyes showed like two drops of blood over his twitching nostrils. He circled swiftly about the end of the lost trail. His nose touched a brown feather, another, and he glided back to the fir tip. A drop of blood was soaking slowly into a dead leaf. The marten thrust his nose into it. One long sniff, while his eyes blazed; then he raised his head, cried out once savagely, and glided away on the back track.

IV. KOOKOOSKOOS, WHO CATCHES THE WRONG RAT.

OOKOOSKOOS is the big brown owl, the *Bubo Virginianus*, or Great Horned Owl of the books. But his Indian name is best. Almost any night in autumn, if you leave the town and go out towards the big woods, you can hear him calling it, *Koo-koo-skoos, koooo, kooo*, down in the swamp.

Kookooskoos is always catching the wrong rat. The reason is that he is a great hunter, and thinks that every furry thing which moves must be game; and so he is like the fool sportsman who shoots at a sound, or a motion in the bushes, before finding out what makes it. Sometimes the rat turns out to be a skunk, or a weasel; sometimes your pet cat; and, once in a lifetime, it is your own fur cap, or even your head; and then you feel the weight and the edge of Kookooskoos' claws. But he never learns wisdom by mistakes; for, spite of his grave appearance, he is excitable as a Frenchman; and so, whenever anything stirs in the bushes and a bit of fur appears, he cries out to himself, *A rat, Kookoo! a rabbit!* and swoops on the instant.

Rats and rabbits are his favorite food, by the way, and he never lets a chance go by of taking them into camp. I think I never climbed to his nest without finding plenty of the fur of both animals to tell of his skill in hunting.

One evening in the twilight, as I came home from hunting in the big woods, I heard the sound of deer feeding just ahead. I stole forward to the edge of a thicket and stood there motionless, looking and listening intently. My cap was in my pocket, and only my head appeared above the low firs that sheltered me. Suddenly, without noise or warning of any kind, I received a sharp blow on the head from behind, as if some one had struck me with a thorny stick. I turned quickly, surprised and a good bit startled; for I thought myself utterly alone in the woods — and I was. There was nobody there. Not a sound, not a motion broke the twilight stillness. Something trickled on my neck; I put up my hand, to find my hair already wet with blood. More startled than ever, I sprang through the thicket, looking, listening everywhere for sight or sound of my enemy. Still no creature bigger than a wood mouse; no movement save that of nodding fir tips; no sound but the thumping of my own heart, and, far behind me, a sudden rush and a bump or two as the frightened deer broke away; then perfect stillness again, as if nothing had ever lived in the thickets.

I was little more than a boy; and I went home that night more puzzled and more frightened than I have ever been, before or since, in the woods. I ran into the doctor's office on my way. He found three cuts in my scalp, and below them two shorter ones, where pointed things seemed to have been driven through to the bone. He looked at me queerly when I told my story. Of course he did not believe me, and I made no effort to persuade him. Indeed, I scarcely believed myself. But for the blood which stained my handkerchief, and the throbbing pain in my head, I should have doubted the reality of the whole experience.

That night I started up out of sleep, some time towards morning, and said before I was half awake: "It was an *owl* that hit you on the head — of course it was an owl!" Then I remembered that, years before, an older boy had a horned owl, which he had taken from a nest, and which he kept loose in a dark garret over the shed. None of us younger boys dared go up to the garret, for the owl was always hungry, and the moment a boy's head appeared through the scuttle the owl said *Hoooo!* and swooped for it. So we used to get acquainted with the big pet by pushing in a dead rat, or a squirrel, or a chicken, on the end of a stick, and climbing in ourselves afterwards.

As I write, the whole picture comes back to me again vividly; the dark, cobwebby old garret, pierced here and there by a pencil of light, in which the motes were dancing; the fierce bird down on the floor in the darkest corner, horns up, eyes gleaming, feathers all a-bristle till he looked big as a bushel basket in the dim light, standing on his game with one foot and tearing it savagely to pieces with the other, snapping his beak and gobbling up feathers, bones and all, in great hungry mouthfuls; and, over the scuttle, two or three small boys staring in eager curiosity, but clinging to each other's coats fearfully, ready to tumble down the ladder with a yell at the first hostile demonstration.

The next afternoon I was back in the big woods to investigate. Fifty feet behind the thicket where I had been struck was a tall dead stub overlooking a

Kookooskoos and the Wrong Rat. 63

little clearing. "That's his watch tower," I thought. "While I was watching the deer, he was up there watching my head, and when it moved he swooped."

I had no intention of giving him another flight at the same game, but hid my fur cap some distance out in the clearing, tied a long string to it, went back into the thicket with the other end of the string, and sat down to wait. A low *Whooo-hoo-hoo!* came from across the valley to tell me I was not the only watcher in the woods.

Towards dusk I noticed suddenly that the top of the old stub looked a bit peculiar, but it was some time before I made out a big owl sitting up there. I had no idea how long he had been there, nor whence he came. His back was towards me; he sat up very straight and still, so as to make himself just a piece, the tip end, of the stub. As I watched, he hooted once and bent forward to listen. Then I pulled on my string.

With the first rustle of a leaf he whirled and poised forward, in the intense attitude an eagle takes when he sights the prey. On the instant he had sighted the cap, wriggling in and out among the low bushes, and swooped for it like an arrow. Just as he dropped his legs to strike, I gave a sharp pull, and the cap jumped from under him. He missed his strike, but wheeled like a fury and struck again. Another jerk, and again he missed. Then he was at the thicket where I stood; his fierce yellow eyes glared straight into mine for a startled instant, and he brushed me with his wings as he sailed away into the shadow of the spruces.

Small doubt now that I had seen my assailant of the night before; for an owl has regular hunting grounds, and uses the same watch towers night after night. He had seen my head in the thicket, and struck at the first movement. Perceiving his mistake, he kept straight on over my head; so of course there was nothing in sight when I turned. As an owl's flight is perfectly noiseless (the wing feathers are wonderfully soft, and all the laminæ are drawn out into hair points, so that the wings never whirr nor rustle like other birds') I had heard nothing, though he passed close enough to strike, and I was listening intently. And so another mystery of the woods was made plain by a little watching.

Years afterwards, the knowledge gained stood me in good stead in clearing up another mystery. It was in a lumber camp — always a superstitious place — in the heart of a Canada forest. I had followed a wandering herd of caribou too far one day, and late in the afternoon found myself alone at a river, some twenty miles from my camp, on the edge of the barren grounds.

Somewhere above me I knew that a crew of lumbermen were at work; so I headed up river to find their camp, if possible, and avoid sleeping out in the snow and bitter cold. It was long after dark, and the moon was flooding forest and river with a wonderful light, when I at last caught sight of the camp. The click of my snowshoes brought a dozen big men to the door. At that moment I felt rather than saw that they seemed troubled and alarmed at seeing me alone; but I was too tired to notice, and no words save those of welcome were spoken until I had eaten heartily. Then, as I started out for another look at the wild beauty of the place under the moonlight, a lumberman followed and touched me on the shoulder.

"Best not go far from camp alone, sir. 'T is n't above safe hereabouts," he said in a low voice. I noticed that he glanced back over his shoulder as he spoke.

"But why?" I objected. "There's nothing in these woods to be afraid of."

"Come back to camp and I'll tell you. It's warmer there," he said. And I followed to hear a strange story,— how "Andy there" was sitting on a stump, smoking his pipe in the twilight, when he was struck and cut on the head from behind; and when he sprang up to look, there was nothing there, nor any track save his own in the snow. The next night Gillie's fur cap had been snatched from his head, and when *he* turned there was nobody in sight; and when he burst into camp, with all his wits frightened out of him, he could scarcely speak, and his face was deathly white. Other uncanny things had happened since, in the same way, and coupled with a bad accident on the river, which the men thought was an omen, they had put the camp into such a state of superstitious fear that no one ventured alone out of doors after nightfall.

I thought of Kookooskoos and my own head, but said nothing. They would only have resented the suggestion.

Next day I found my caribou, and returned to the lumber camp before sunset. At twilight there was Kookooskoos, an enormous fellow, looking like the end of a big spruce stub, keeping sharp watch over the clearing, and fortunately behind the camp where he could not see the door. I called the men and set them crouching in the snow under the low eaves.— "Stay there a minute and I'll show you the ghost." That was all I told them.

Taking the skin of a hare which I had shot that day, I hoisted it cautiously on a stick, the lumbermen watching curiously. A slight scratch of the stick, a movement of the fur along the splits, then a great dark shadow shot over our heads. It struck the stick sharply and swept on and up into the spruces across the clearing, taking Bunny's skin with it.

Then one big lumberman, who saw the point, jumped up with a yell and danced a jig in the snow, like a schoolboy. There was no need of further demonstration with a cap; and nobody volunteered his head for a final experiment; but all remembered seeing the owl on his nightly watch, and knew something of his swooping habits. Of course some were incredulous at first, and had a dozen questions and objections when we were in camp. No one likes to have a good ghost story spoiled; and, besides, where superstition is, there the marvelous is most easily believed. It is only the simple truth that is doubted. So I spent half the night in convincing them that they *had* been brought up in the woods to be scared by an owl.

Poor Kookooskoos! they shot him next night on his watch tower, and nailed him to the camp door as a warning.

I discovered another curious thing about Kookooskoos that night when I watched to find out what had struck me. I found out why he hoots. Sometimes, if he is a young owl, he hoots for practice, or to learn how; and then he makes an awful noise of it, a rasping screech, before his voice deepens. And if you are camping near and are new to the woods, the chances are that you lie awake and shiver; for there is no other sound like it in the wilderness. Sometimes, when you climb to his nest, he has a terrifying *hoo-hoo-hoo-hoo-hoo-hoo*, running up and down a deep guttural scale, like a fiendish laugh, accompanied by a vicious snapping of the beak. And if you are a small boy, and it is towards twilight, you climb down the tree quick and let his nest alone. But the regular *whooo-hoo-hoo, whooo-hoo*, always five notes, with the second two very short, is a hunting call, and he uses it to alarm the game. That is queer hunting; but his ears account for it.

If you separate the feathers on Kookooskoos' head, you will find an enormous ear-opening running from above his eye halfway round his face. And the ear within is so marvelously sensitive that it can hear the rustle of a rat in the grass, or the scrape of a sparrow's toes on a branch fifty feet away. So he sits on his watch tower, so still that he is never noticed, and as twilight comes on, when he can see best, he hoots suddenly and listens. The sound has a muffled quality which makes it hard to locate, and it frightens every bird and small animal within hearing; for all know Kookooskoos, and how fierce he is. As the terrifying sound rolls out of the air so near them, fur

Kookooskoos and the Wrong Rat.

and feathers shiver with fright. A rabbit stirs in his form; a partridge shakes on his branch; the mink stops hunting frogs at the brook; the skunk takes his nose out of the hole where he is eating sarsaparilla roots. A leaf stirs, a toe scrapes, and instantly Kookooskoos is there. His fierce eyes glare in; his great claws drop; one grip, and it's all over. For the very sight of him scares the little creatures so, that there is no life left in them to cry out or to run away.

A nest which I found a few years ago shows how well this kind of hunting succeeds. It was in a gloomy evergreen swamp, in a big tree, some eighty feet from the ground. I found it by a pile of pellets of hair and feathers at the foot of the tree; for the owl devours every part of his game, and after digestion is complete, feathers, bones, and hair are disgorged in small balls, like so many sparrow heads. When I looked up, there at the top was a huge mass of sticks, which had been added to year after year till it was nearly three feet across, and half as thick. Kookooskoos was not there. He had heard me coming and slipped away silently.

Wishing to be sure the nest was occupied before trying the hard climb, I went away as far as I could see the nest and hid in a thicket. Presently a very large owl came back and stood by the nest. Soon after, a smaller bird, the male, glided up beside her. Then I came on cautiously, watching to see what they would do.

At the first crack of a twig both birds started forward; the male slipped away; the female dropped below the nest, and stood behind a limb, just her face peering through a crotch in my direction. Had I not known she was there, I might have looked the tree over twenty times without finding her. And there she stayed hidden till I was halfway up the tree.

When I peered at last over the edge of the big nest, after a desperately hard climb, there was a bundle of dark gray down in a little hollow in the middle. It touched me at the time that the little ones rested on a feather bed pulled from the mother bird's own breast. I brushed the down with my fingers. Instantly, two heads came up, fuzzy gray heads, with black pointed beaks, and beautiful hazel eyes, and a funny long pin-feather over each ear, which made them look like little wise old clerks just waked up. When I touched them again they staggered up and opened their mouths,—enormous mouths for such little fellows; then, seeing that I was an intruder, they tried to bristle their few pin-feathers and snap their beaks.

They were fat as two aldermen; and no wonder.

Placed around the edge of the big nest were a red squirrel, a rat, a chicken, a few frogs' legs, and a rabbit. Fine fare that, at eighty feet from the ground. Kookooskoos had had good hunting. All the game was partly eaten, showing I had disturbed their dinner; and only the hinder parts were left, showing that owls like the head and brains best. I left them undisturbed and came away; for I wanted to watch the young grow — which they did marvelously, and were presently learning to hoot. But I have been less merciful to the great owls ever since, thinking of the enormous destruction of game represented in raising two or three such young savages, year after year, in the same swamp.

Once, at twilight, I shot a big owl that was sitting on a limb facing me, with what appeared to be an enormously long tail hanging below the limb. The tail turned out to be a large mink, just killed, with a beautiful skin that put five dollars into a boy's locker. Another time I shot one that sailed over me; when he came down, there was a ruffed grouse, still living, in his claws. Another time I could not touch one that I had killed for the overpowering odor which was in his feathers, showing that *Mephitis*, the skunk, never loses his head when attacked. But Kookooskoos, like the fox, cares little for such weapons, and in the spring, when game is scarce, swoops for and kills a skunk wherever he finds him prowling away from his den in the twilight.

The most savage bit of his hunting that I ever saw was one dark winter afternoon, on the edge of some thick woods. I was watching a cat, a half-wild creature, that was watching a red squirrel making a great fuss over some nuts which he had hidden, and which he claimed somebody had stolen. Somewhere behind us, Kookooskoos was watching from a pine tree. The squirrel was chattering in the midst of a whirlwind of leaves and empty shells which he had thrown out on the snow from under the wall; behind him the cat, creeping nearer and nearer, had crouched with blazing eyes and quivering muscles, her whole attention fixed on the spring, when broad wings shot silently over my hiding place and fell like a shadow on the cat. One set of strong claws gripped her behind the ears; the others were fastened like a vise in the spine. Generally one such grip is enough; but the cat was strong, and at the first touch sprang away. In a moment the owl was after her, floating, hovering above, till the right moment came, when he dropped and struck again. Then the cat whirled and fought like a fury. For a few moments there was a desperate battle, fur and feathers flying, the cat screeching like mad, the owl silent as death. Then the great claws did their work. When I straightened up from my thicket, Kookooskoos was standing on his game, tearing off the flesh with his feet, and carrying it up to his mouth with the same movement, swallowing everything alike, as if famished.

Over them the squirrel, which had whisked up a tree at the first alarm, was peeking with evil eyes over the edge of a limb, snickering at the blood-stained snow and the dead cat, scolding, barking, threatening the owl for having disturbed the search for his stolen walnuts.

I caught that same owl soon after in a peculiar way. A farmer near by told me that an owl was taking his chickens regularly. Undoubtedly the bird had been driven southward by the severe winter, and had not taken up regular hunting grounds until he caught the cat. Then came the chickens. I set up a pole, on the top of which was nailed a bit of board for a platform. On the platform was fastened a small steel trap, and under it hung a dead chicken. The next morning there was Kookooskoos on the platform, one foot in the trap, at which he was pulling awkwardly. Owls, from their peculiar ways of hunting, are prone to light on stubs and exposed branches; and so Kookooskoos had used my pole as a watch tower before carrying off his game.

There is another way in which he is easily fooled. In the early spring, when he is mating, and again in the autumn, when the young birds are well fed and before they have learned much, you can bring him close up to you by imitating his hunting call. In the wilderness, where these birds are plenty, I have often had five or six about me at once. You have only to go well out beyond your tent, and sit down quietly, making yourself part of the place. Give the call a few times, and if there is a young bird near with a full stomach, he will answer, and presently come nearer. Soon he is in the tree over your head, and if you keep perfectly still he will set up a great hooting that you have called him and now do not answer. Others are attracted by his calling; they come in silently from all directions; the outcry is startling. The call is more nervous, more eerie, much more terrifying close at hand than when heard in the distance. They sweep about like great dark shadows, hoo-hoo-hooing and frolicking in their own uncanny way; then go off to their separate watch towers and their hunting. But the chances are that you will be awakened with a start more than once in the night, as some inquisitive young owl comes back and gives the hunting call in the hope of finding out what the first summons was all about.

V. CHIGWOOLTZ THE FROG.

I WAS watching for a bear one day by an alder point, when Chigwooltz came swimming in from the lily pads in great curiosity to see what I was doing under the alders. He was an enormous frog, dull green with a yellowish vest — which showed that he was a male — but with the most brilliant ear drums I had ever seen. They fairly glowed with iridescent color, each in its ring of bright yellow. When I tried to catch him (very quietly, for the bear was somewhere just above on the ridge) in order to examine these drums, he dived under the canoe and watched me from a distance.

In front of me, in the shallow water along shore, four more large frogs were sunning themselves among the lily pads. I watched them carelessly while waiting for the bear. After an hour or two I noticed that three of these frogs changed their positions slightly, turning from time to time so as to warm the entire body at nature's fireplace. But the fourth was more deliberate and philosophical, thinking evidently that if he simply sat still long enough the sun would do the turning. When I came, about eleven o'clock, he was sitting on the shore by a green stone, his fore feet lapped by tiny ripples, the sun full on his back. For three hours, while I watched there, he never moved a muscle. Then the bear came, and I left him for more exciting things.

Late in the afternoon I came back to get some of the big frogs for breakfast. Chigwooltz, he with the ear drums, was the first to see me, and came pushing his way among the lily pads toward the canoe. But when I dangled a red ibis fly in front of him, he dived promptly, and I saw his head come up by a black root, where he sat, thinking himself invisible, and watched me.

Chigwooltz the second, he of the green stone and the patient disposition, was still sitting in the same place. The sun had turned round; it was now warming his other side. His all-day sun bath surprised me so that I let him alone, to see how long he would sit still, and went fishing for other frogs.

Two big ones showed their heads among the pads some twenty feet apart. Pushing up so as to make a triangle with my canoe, I dangled a red ibis impartially between them. For two or three long minutes neither moved so much as an eyelid. Then one seemed to wake suddenly from a trance, or to be touched by an electric wire, for he came scrambling in a desperate hurry over the lily pads. Swimming was too slow; he jumped fiercely out of water at the red challenge, making a great splash and commotion.

Fishing for big frogs, by the way, is no tame sport. The red seems to excite them tremendously, and they take the fly like a black salmon.

But the moment the first frog started, frog number two waked up and darted forward, making less noise but coming more swiftly. The first frog had jumped once for the fly and missed it, when the other leaped upon him savagely, and a fight began, while the ibis lay neglected on a lily pad. They pawed and bit each other fiercely for several minutes; then the second frog, a little smaller than the other, got the grip he wanted and held it. He clasped his fore legs tight about his rival's neck and began to strangle him slowly. I knew well how strong Chigwooltz is in his forearms, and that his fightings and wrestlings are desperate affairs; but I did not know till then how savage he can be. He had gripped from behind by a clever dive, so as to use his weight when the right moment came. Tighter and tighter he hugged; the big frog's eyes seemed bursting from his head, and his mouth was forced slowly open. Then his savage opponent lunged upon him with his weight, and forced his head under water to finish him.

The whole thing seemed scarcely more startling to the luckless big frog than to the watcher in the canoe. It was all so brutal, so deliberately planned! The smaller frog, knowing that he was no match for the other in strength, had waited cunningly till he was all absorbed in the red fly, and then stole upon him, intending to finish him first and the little red thing afterwards. He would have done it too; for the big frog was at his last gasp, when I interfered and put them both in my net.

Meanwhile a third frog had come *walloping* over the lily pads from somewhere out of sight, and grabbed the fly while the other two were fighting about it. It was he who first showed me a curious frog trick. When I lifted him from the water on the end of my line, he raised his hands above his head, as if he had been a man, and grasped the line, and tried to lift himself, hand over hand, so as to take the strain from his mouth. — And I could never catch another frog like that.

Next morning, as I went to the early fishing, Chigwooltz, the patient, sat by the same stone, his fore feet at the edge of the same bronze lily leaf. At noon he was still there; in twenty-four hours at least he had not moved a muscle.

At twilight I was following a bear along the shore. It was the restless season, when bears are moving constantly; scarcely a twilight passed that I did not meet one or more on their wanderings. This one was heading for the upper end of the lake, traveling in the shallow water near shore; and I was just behind him, stealing along in my canoe to see what queer thing he would do. He was in no hurry, as most other bears were, but went nosing along shore, acting much as a fat pig would in the same place. As he approached the alder point he stopped suddenly, and twisted his head a bit, and set his ears, as a dog does that sees something very interesting. Then he began to steal forward. Could it be — I shot my canoe forward — yes, it was Chigwooltz, still sitting by the green stone, with his eye, like Bunsby's, on the coast of Greenland. In thirty-two hours, to my knowledge, he had not stirred.

Mooween the bear crept nearer; he was crouching now like a cat, stealing along in the soft mud behind Chigwooltz so as to surprise him. I saw him raise one paw slowly, cautiously, high above his head.

Down it came, *souse!* sending up a shower of mud and water. And Chigwooltz the restful, who could sit still thirty-two hours without getting stiff in the joints, and then dodge the sweep of Mooween's paw, went splashing away *hippety-ippety* over the lily pads to some water grass, where he said *K'tung!* and disappeared for good.

A few days later Simmo and I moved camp to a grove of birches just above the alder point. From behind my tent an old game path led down to the bay where the big frogs lived. There were scores of them there; the chorus at night, with its multitude of voices running from a whistling treble to deep, deep bass, was at times tremendous. It was here that I had the first good opportunity of watching frogs feeding.

Chigwooltz, I found, is a perfect gourmand and a cannibal, eating, besides his regular diet of flies and beetles and water snails, young frogs, and crawfish, and turtles, and fish of every kind. But few have ever seen him at his hunting, for he is active only at night or on dark days.

I used to watch them from the shore or from my canoe at twilight. Just outside the lily pads a shoal of minnows would be playing at the surface, or small trout would be rising freely for the night insects.

Chigwooltz the Frog.

Then, if you watched sharply, you would see gleaming points of light, the eyes of Chigwooltz, stealing out, with barely a ripple, to the edge of the pads. And then, when some big feeding trout drove the minnows or small fry close in, there would be a heavy plunge from the shadow of the pads; and you would hear Chigwooltz splashing if the fish were a larger one than he expected.

That is why small frogs are so deadly afraid if you take them outside the fringe of lily pads. They know that big hungry trout feed in from the deeps, and that big frogs, savage cannibals every one, watch out from the shadowy fringe of water plants. If you drop a little frog there, in clear water, he will shoot in as fast as his frightened legs will drive him, swimming first on top to avoid fish, diving deep as he reaches the pads to avoid his hungry relatives; and so in to shallow water and thick stems, where he can dodge about and the big frogs cannot follow.

All sorts and conditions of frogs lived in that little bay. There was one inquisitive fellow, who always came out of the pads and swam as near as he could get whenever I appeared on the shore. Another would sit in his favorite spot, under a stranded log, and let me come as close as I would; but the moment I dangled the red ibis fly in front of him, he would disappear like a wink, and not show himself again. Another would follow the fly in a wild kangaroo dance over the lily pads, going round and round the canoe as if bewitched, and would do his best to climb in after the bit of color when I pulled it up slowly over the bark. He afforded me so much good fun that I could not eat him; though I always stopped to give him another dance, whenever I went fishing for other frogs just like him. Further along shore lived another, a perfect savage, so wild that I could never catch him, which strangled or drowned two big frogs in a week, to my certain knowledge. And then, one night when I was trying to find my canoe which I had lost in the darkness, I came upon a frog migration, dozens and dozens of them, all hopping briskly in the same direction. They had left the stream, driven by some strange instinct, just like rats or squirrels, and were going through the woods to the unknown destination that beckoned them so strongly that they could not but follow.

The most curious and interesting bit of their strange life came out at night, when they were fascinated by my light. I used sometimes to set a candle on a piece of board for a float, and place it in the water close to shore, where the ripples would set it dancing gently. Then I would place a little screen

Never a word was spoken: the silence was perfect

of bark at the shore end of the float, and sit down behind it in darkness.

Presently two points of light would begin to shine, then to scintillate, out among the lily pads, and Chigwooltz would come stealing in, his eyes growing bigger and brighter with wonder. He would place his forearms akimbo on the edge of the float, and lift himself up a bit, like a little old man, and stare steadfastly at the light. And there he would stay as long as I let him, just staring and blinking.

Soon two other points of light would come stealing in from the other side, and another frog would set his elbows on the float and stare hard across at the first-comer. And then two more shining points, and two more, till twelve or fifteen frogs were gathered about my beacon, as thick as they could find elbow room on the float, all staring and blinking like so many strange water owls come up from the bottom to debate weighty things, with a little flickering will-o'-the-wisp nodding grave assent in the midst of them. But never a word was spoken; the silence was perfect.

Sometimes one, more fascinated or more curious than the others, would climb onto the float, and put his nose solemnly into the light. Then there would be a loud sizzle, a jump, and a splash; the candle would go out, and the wondering circle of frogs scatter to the lily pads again, all swimming as if in a trance, dipping their heads under water to wash the light from their bewildered eyes.

They were quite fearless, almost senseless, at such times. I would stretch out my hand from the shadow, pick up an unresisting frog that threatened too soon to climb onto the float, and examine him at leisure. But Chigwooltz is wedded to his idols; the moment I released him he would go, fast as his legs could carry him, to put his elbows on the float and stare at the light again.

Among the frogs, and especially among the toads, as among most wild animals, certain individuals attach themselves strongly to man, drawn doubtless by some unknown but no less strongly felt attraction. It was so there in the wilderness. The first morning after our arrival at the birch grove I was down at the shore, preparing a trout for baking in the ashes, when Chigwooltz, of the ear drums, biggest of all the frogs, came from among the lily pads. He had lost all fear apparently; he swam directly up to me, touching my hands with his nose, and even crawling out to my feet in the greatest curiosity.

After that he took up his abode near the foot of the game path. I had only to splash the water there with my finger when he would come from beside a green stone, or from under a log or the lily pads — for he had a dozen hiding places — and swim up to me to be fed, or petted, or to have his back scratched.

He ate all sorts of things, insects, bread, beef, game and fish, either raw or cooked. I would attach a bit of meat to a string or straw, and wiggle it before him, to make it seem alive. The moment he saw it (he had a queer way sometimes of staring hard at a thing without seeing it) he would crouch and creep towards it, nearer and nearer, softly and more softly, like a cat stalking a chipmunk. Then there would be a red flash and the meat would be gone. The red flash was his tongue, which is attached at the outer end and folds back in his mouth. It is, moreover, large and sticky, and he can throw it out and back like lightning. All you see is the red flash of it, and his game is gone.

One day, to try the effects of nicotine on a new subject, I took a bit of Simmo's black tobacco and gave it to Chigwooltz. He ate it thankfully, as he did everything else I gave him. In a little while he grew uneasy, sitting up and rubbing his belly with his fore paws. Presently he brought his stomach up into his mouth, turned it inside out to get rid of the tobacco, washed it thoroughly in the lake, swallowed it down again, and was ready for his bread and beef.

A most convenient arrangement that; and also a perfectly unbiased opinion on a much debated subject.

Chigwooltz, unlike many of my pets, was not in the least dependent on my bounty. Indeed, he was a remarkable hunter on his own account, and what he took from me he took as hospitality, not charity. One morning he came to me with the tail of a small trout sticking out of his mouth. The rest of the fish was below, being digested. Another day, towards twilight, I saw him resting on the lily pads, looking very full, with a suspicious-looking object curling out over his under lip. I wiggled my finger in the water, and he came from pure sociability, for he was beyond eating any more. The suspicious-looking object proved to be a bird's foot, and beside it was a pointed wing tip. That was too much for my curiosity. I opened his mouth and pulled out the bird with some difficulty, for Chigwooltz had been engaged some time in the act of swallowing his game and had it well down. It proved to be a full-grown male swallow, without a mark anywhere to show how he had come by his death. Chigwooltz looked at me reproachfully, but swallowed his game promptly the moment I had finished examining it.

There was small doubt in my mind that he had caught his bird fairly, by a quick spring as the swallow

Chigwooltz the Frog.

touched the water almost at his nose, near one of his numerous lurking places. Still it puzzled me a good deal till one early morning, when I saw him in broad daylight do a much more difficult thing than snapping up a swallow.

I was coming down the game path to the shore when a bird, a tree sparrow I thought, flew to the ground just ahead of me, and hopped to the water to drink. I watched him a moment curiously, then with intense interest as I saw a ripple steal out of the lily pads towards him. The ripple was Chigwooltz.

The sparrow had finished drinking and was absorbed in a morning bath. Chigwooltz stole nearer and nearer, sinking himself till only his eyes showed above water. The ripple that flowed away on either side was gentle as that of a floating leaf. Then, just as the bird had sipped and lifted its head for a last swallow, Chigwooltz hurled himself out of water. One snap of his big mouth, and the sparrow was done for.

An hour later, when I came down to my canoe, he was sitting low on the lily pads, winking sleepily now and then, with eight little sparrow's toes curling over the rim of his under lip, like a hornpout's whiskers.

VI. CLOUD WINGS THE EAGLE.

"HERE he is again! here's Old Whitehead, robbing the fish-hawk."

I started up from the little *commoosie* beyond the fire, at Gillie's excited cry, and ran to join him on the shore. A glance out over Caribou Point to the big bay, where innumerable whitefish were shoaling, showed me another chapter in a long but always interesting story. Ismaquehs, the fish-hawk, had risen from the lake with a big fish, and was doing his best to get away to his nest, where his young ones were clamoring. Over him soared the eagle, still as fate and as sure, now dropping to flap a wing in Ismaquehs' face, now touching him with his great talons gently, as if to say, "Do you feel that, Ismaquehs? If I grip once 't will be the end of you and your fish together. And what will the little ones do then, up in the nest on

There he poised on dark broad wings

the old pine? Better drop him peacefully; you can catch another.—*Drop him!* I say."

Up to that moment the eagle had merely bothered the big hawk's flight, with a gentle reminder now and then that he meant no harm, but wanted the fish which he could not catch himself. Now there was a change, a flash of the king's temper. With a roar of wings he whirled round the hawk like a tempest, bringing up short and fierce, squarely in his line of flight. There he poised on dark broad wings, his yellow eyes glaring fiercely into the shrinking soul of Ismaquehs, his talons drawn hard back for a deadly strike. And Simmo the Indian, who had run down to join me, muttered: "Cheplahgan mad now. Ismaquehs find-um out in a minute."

But Ismaquehs knew just when to stop. With a cry of rage he dropped, or rather threw, his fish, hoping it would strike the water and be lost. On the instant the eagle wheeled out of the way and bent his head sharply. I had seen him fold wings and drop before, and had held my breath at the speed. But dropping was of no use now, for the fish fell faster. Instead he swooped downward, adding to the weight of his fall the push of his strong wings, glancing down like a bolt to catch the fish ere it struck the water, and rising again in a great curve — up and away steadily, evenly as the king should fly, to his own little ones far away on the mountain.

Weeks before, I had had my introduction to Old Whitehead, as Gillie called him, on the Madawaska. We were pushing up river on our way to the wilderness, when a great outcry and the *bang-bang* of a gun sounded just ahead. Dashing round a wooded bend, we came upon a man with a smoking gun, a boy up to his middle in the river, trying to get across, and, on the other side, a black sheep running about *baaing* at every jump.

"He's taken the lamb; he's taken the lamb!" shouted the boy. Following the direction of his pointing finger, I saw Old Whitehead, a splendid bird, rising heavily above the tree-tops across the clearing. Reaching back almost instinctively, I clutched the heavy rifle which Gillie put into my hand and jumped out of the canoe; for with a rifle one wants steady footing. It was a long shot, but not so very difficult; Old Whitehead had got his bearings and was moving steadily, straight away. A second after the report of the rifle, we saw him hitch and swerve in the air; then two white quills came floating down, and as he turned we saw the break in his broad white tail. And that was the mark that we knew him by ever afterwards.

That was nearly eighty miles by canoe from where we now stood, though scarcely ten in a straight line over the mountains; for the rivers and lakes we were following doubled back almost to the starting point; and the whole wild, splendid country was the eagle's hunting ground. Wherever I went I saw him, following the rivers for stranded trout and salmon, or floating high in air where he could overlook two or three wilderness lakes, with as many honest fish-hawks catching their dinners. I had promised the curator of a museum that I would get him an eagle that summer, and so took to hunting the great bird diligently. But hunting was of little use, except to teach me many of his ways and habits; for he seemed to have eyes and ears all over him; and whether I crept like a snake through the woods, or floated like a wild duck in my canoe over the water, he always saw or heard me, and was off before I could get within shooting distance.

Then I tried to trap him. I placed two large trout, with a steel trap between them, in a shallow spot on the river that I could watch from my camp on a bluff, half a mile below. Next day Gillie, who was more eager than I, set up a shout; and running out I saw Old Whitehead standing in the shallows and flopping about the trap. We jumped into a canoe and pushed up river in hot haste, singing in exultation that we had the fierce old bird at last. When we doubled the last point that hid the shallows, there was Old Whitehead, still tugging away at a fish, and splashing the water not thirty yards away. I shall not soon forget his attitude and expression as we shot round the point, his body erect and rigid, his wings half spread, his head thrust forward, eyelids drawn straight, and a strong fierce gleam of freedom and utter wildness in his bright eyes. So he stood, a magnificent creature, till we were almost upon him,—when he rose quietly, taking one of the trout. The other was already in his stomach. He was not in the trap at all, but had walked carefully round it. The splashing was made in tearing one fish to pieces with his claws, and freeing the other from a stake that held it.

After that he would not go near the shallows; for a new experience had come into his life, leaving its shadow dark behind it. He who was king of all he surveyed from the old blasted pine on the crag's top, who had always heretofore been the hunter, now knew what it meant to be hunted. And the fear of it was in his eyes, I think, and softened their fierce gleam when I looked into them again, weeks later, by his own nest on the mountain.

Simmo entered also into our hunting, but without

enthusiasm or confidence. He had chased the same eagle before — all one summer, in fact, when a sportsman, whom he was guiding, had offered him twenty dollars for the royal bird's skin. But Old Whitehead still wore it triumphantly; and Simmo prophesied for him long life and a natural death. "No use hunt-um dat heagle," he said simply. "I try once an' can't get near him. He see everyt'ing; and wot he don't see, he hear. 'Sides, he kin *feel* danger. Das why he build nest way off, long ways, O don' know where." This last with a wave of his arm to include the universe. Cheplahgan, Old Cloud Wings, he proudly called the bird that had defied him in a summer's hunting.

At first I had hunted him like any other savage; partly, of course, to get his skin for the curator; partly, perhaps, to save the settler's lambs over on the Madawaska; but chiefly just to kill him, to exult in his death flaps, and to rid the woods of a cruel tyrant. Gradually, however, a change came over me as I hunted; I sought him less and less for his skin and his life, and more and more for himself, to know all about him. I used to watch him by the hour from my camp on the big lake, sailing quietly over Caribou Point, after he had eaten with his little ones, and was disposed to let Ismaquehs go on with his fishing in peace. He would set his great wings to the breeze and sit like a kite in the wind, mounting steadily in an immense spiral, up and up, without the shadow of effort, till the eye grew dizzy in following. And I loved to watch him, so strong, so free, so sure of himself — round and round, up and ever up, without hurry, without exertion; and every turn found the heavens nearer and the earth spread wider below. Now head and tail gleam silver white in the sunshine; now he hangs motionless, a cross of jet that a lady might wear at her throat, against the clear, unfathomable blue of the June heavens — there! he is lost in the blue, so high that I cannot see any more. But even as I turn away he plunges down into vision again, dropping with folded wings straight down like a plummet, faster and faster, larger and larger, through a terrifying rush of air, till I spring to my feet and catch the breath, as if I myself were falling. And just before he dashes himself to pieces he turns in the air, head downward, and half spreads his wings, and goes shooting, slanting down towards the lake, then up in a great curve to the tree-tops, where he can watch better what Kakagos, the rare woods-raven, is doing, and what game he is hunting. For that is what Cheplahgan came down in such a hurry to find out about.

Again he would come in the early morning, sweeping up river as if he had already been a long day's journey, with the air of far-away and far-to-go in his onward rush. And if I were at the trout pools, and very still, I would hear the strong silken rustle of his wings as he passed. At midday I would see him poised over the highest mountain-top northward, at an enormous altitude, where the imagination itself could not follow the splendid sweep of his vision; and at evening he would cross the lake, moving westward into the sunset on tireless pinions — always strong, noble, magnificent in his power and loneliness, a perfect emblem of the great lonely magnificent wilderness.

One day as I watched him, it swept over me suddenly that forest and river would be incomplete without him. The thought of this came back to me, and spared him to the wilderness, on the last occasion when I went hunting for his life.

That was just after we reached the big lake, where I saw him robbing the fish-hawk. After much searching and watching I found a great log by the outlet where Old Whitehead often perched. There was a big eddy hard by, on the edge of a shallow, and he used to sit on the log, waiting for fish to come out where he could wade in and get them. There was a sickness among the suckers that year (it comes regularly every few years, as among rabbits), and they would come struggling out of the deep water to rest on the sand, only to be caught by the minks and fish-hawks and bears and Old Whitehead, all of whom were waiting and hungry for fish.

For several days I put a big bait of trout and whitefish on the edge of the shallows. The first two baits were put out late in the afternoon, and a bear got them both the next night. Then I put them out in the early morning, and before noon Cheplahgan had found them. He came straight as a string from his watch place over the mountain, miles away, causing me to wonder greatly what strange sixth sense guided him; for sight and smell seemed equally out of the question. The next day he came again. Then I placed the best bait of all in the shallows, and hid in the dense underbrush near, with my gun.

He came at last, after hours of waiting, dropping from above the tree-tops with a heavy rustling of pinions. And as he touched the old log, and spread his broad white tail, I saw and was proud of the gap which my bullet had made weeks before. He stood there a moment erect and splendid, head, neck, and tail a shining white; even the dark brown feathers of his body glinted in the bright sunshine. And he turned his head slowly from side to side, his keen eyes flashing, as if he would say, " Behold, a king!" to Chigwooltz the frog, and Tookhees the wood mouse, and to any other chance wild creature that might watch him from the underbrush at his unkingly act of feeding on dead fish. Then he hopped down — rather awkwardly, it must be confessed; for he is a creature of the upper deeps, who cannot bear to touch the earth — seized a fish, which he tore to pieces with his claws and ate greedily. Twice I tried to shoot him; but the thought of the wilderness without him was upon me, and held me back. Then, too, it seemed so mean to pot him from ambush when he had come down to earth, where he was at a disadvantage; and when he clutched some of the larger fish in his talons, and rose swiftly and bore away westward, all desire to kill him was gone. There were little Cloud Wings, it seemed, which I must also find and watch. After that I hunted him more diligently than before, but without my gun. And a curious desire, which I could not account for, took possession of me: to touch this untamed, untouched creature of the clouds and mountains.

Next day I did it. There were thick bushes growing along one end of the old log on which the eagle rested. Into these I cut a tunnel with my hunting-knife, arranging the tops in such a way as to screen me more effectively. Then I put out my bait, a good two hours before the time of Old Whitehead's earliest appearance, and crawled into my den to wait.

I had barely settled comfortably into my place, wondering how long human patience could endure the sting of insects and the hot close air without moving or stirring a leaf, when the heavy silken rustle sounded close at hand, and I heard the grip of his talons on the log. There he stood, at arm's length, turning his head uneasily, the light glinting on his white crest, the fierce, untamed flash in his bright eye. Never before had he seemed so big, so strong, so splendid; my heart jumped at the thought of him as our national emblem. I am glad still to have seen that emblem once, and felt the thrill of it.

But I had little time to think, for Cheplahgan was restless. Some instinct seemed to warn him of a danger that he could not see. The moment his head was turned away, I stretched out my arm. Scarcely a leaf moved with the motion, yet he whirled like a flash and crouched to spring, his eyes glaring straight into mine with an intensity that I could scarce endure. Perhaps I was mistaken, but in that swift instant the hard glare in his eyes seemed to soften with fear, as he recognized me as the one thing in the wilderness that dared to hunt him, the king. My hand touched him fair on the shoulder; then he shot into the air, and went sweeping in great circles over the tree-tops, still looking down at the man, wondering and fearing at the way in which he had been brought into the man's power.

But one thing he did not understand. Standing erect on the log, and looking up at him as he swept over me, I kept thinking, "I did it, I did it, Cheplahgan, old Cloud Wings. And I had grabbed your legs, and pinned you down, and tied you in a bag, and brought you to camp, but that I chose to let you go free. And that is better than shooting you. Now I shall find your little ones and touch them too."

For several days I had been watching Old Whitehead's lines of flight, and had concluded that his nest was somewhere in the hills northwest of the big lake. I went there one afternoon, and while confused in the big timber, which gave no outlook in any direction, I saw, not Old Whitehead, but a larger eagle, his mate undoubtedly, flying straight westward with food towards a great cliff, that I had noticed with my glass one day from a mountain on the other side of the lake.

When I went there, early next morning, it was Cheplahgan himself who showed me where his nest was. I was hunting along the foot of the cliff when, glancing back towards the lake, I saw him coming far away, and hid in the underbrush. He passed very near, and following, I saw him standing on a ledge near the top of the cliff. Just below him, in the top of a stunted tree growing out of the face of the rock, was a huge mass of sticks that formed the nest, with a great mother-eagle standing by, feeding the little ones. Both birds started away silently when I appeared, but came back soon and swept back and forth over me, as I sat watching the nest and the face of the cliff through my glass. No need now of caution. Both birds seemed to know instinctively why I had come, and that the fate of the eaglets lay in my hands if I could but scale the cliff.

It was scaring business, that three-hundred-foot climb up the sheer face of the mountain. Fortunately the rock was seamed and scarred with the wear of centuries; bushes and stunted trees grew out of countless crevices, which gave me sure footing, and sometimes a lift of a dozen feet or more on my way up. As I climbed, the eagles circled lower and lower; the strong rustling of their wings was about my head continually; they seemed to grow larger, fiercer, every moment, as my hold grew more precarious, and the earth and the pointed tree-tops dropped farther below. There was a good revolver in my pocket, to use in case of necessity; but had the

Cloud Wings the Eagle.

great birds attacked me I should have fared badly, for at times I was obliged to grip hard with both hands, my face to the cliff, leaving the eagles free to strike from above and behind. I think now that had I shown fear in such a place, or shouted, or tried to fray them away, they would have swooped upon me, wing and claw, like furies. I could see it in their fierce eyes as I looked up. But the thought of the times when I had hunted him, and especially the thought of that time when I had reached out of the bushes and touched him, was upon Old Whitehead and made him fear. So I kept steadily on my way, apparently giving no thought to the eagles, though deep inside I was anxious enough, and reached the foot of the tree in which the nest was made.

I stood there a long time, my arm clasping the twisted old boll, looking out over the forest spread wide below, partly to regain courage, partly to reassure the eagles, which were circling very near with a kind of intense wonder in their eyes, but chiefly to make up my mind what to do next. The tree was easy to climb, but the nest — a huge affair, which had been added to year after year — filled the whole tree-top, and I could gain no foothold, from which to look over and see the eaglets, without tearing the nest to pieces. I did not want to do that, and I doubted whether the mother-eagle would stand it. A dozen times she seemed on the point of dropping on my head to tear it with her talons; but always she veered off as I looked up quietly, and Old Whitehead, with the mark of my bullet strong upon him, swept between her and me and seemed to say, "Wait, wait. I don't understand; but he can kill us if he will — and the little ones are in his power." Now he was closer to me than ever, and the fear was vanishing. But so also was the fierceness.

From the foot of the tree the crevice in which it grew led upwards to the right, then doubled back to the ledge above the nest, upon which Cheplahgan was standing when I discovered him. The lip of this crevice made a dizzy path that one might follow by moving crabwise, his face to the cliff, with only its roughnesses to cling to with his fingers. I tried it at last, crept up and out twenty feet, and back ten, and dropped with a great breath of relief to a broad ledge covered with bones and fish scales, the relics of many a savage feast. Below me, almost within reach, was the nest, with two dark, scraggly young birds resting on twigs and grass, with fish, flesh and fowl in a gory, skinny, scaly ring about them — the most savage-looking household into which I ever looked unbidden.

Cloud Wings the Eagle.

But even as I looked and wondered, and tried to make out what other game had been furnished the young savages I had helped to feed, a strange thing happened, which touched me as few things ever have among the wild creatures. The eagles had followed me close along the last edge of rock, hoping no doubt in their wild hearts that I would slip, and end their troubles, and give my body as food to the young. Now, as I sat on the ledge, peering eagerly into the nest, the great mother-bird left me and hovered over her eaglets, as if to shield them with her wings from even the sight of my eyes. But Old Whitehead still circled over me. Lower he came, and lower, till with a supreme effort of daring he folded his wings and dropped to the ledge beside me, within ten feet, and turned and looked into my eyes. "See," he seemed to say, "we are within reach again. You touched me once; I don't know how or why. Here I am now, to touch or to kill, as you will; only spare the little ones."

A moment later the mother-bird dropped to the edge of the nest. And there we sat, we three, with the wonder upon us all, the young eagles at our feet, the cliff above, and, three hundred feet below, the spruce tops of the wilderness reaching out and away to the mountains beyond the big lake.

I sat perfectly still, which is the only way to reassure a wild creature; and soon I thought Cheplahgan had lost his fear in his anxiety for the little ones. But the moment I rose to go he was in the air again, circling restlessly above my head with his mate, the same wild fierceness in his eyes as he looked down. A half-hour later I had gained the top of the cliff and started eastward towards the lake, coming down by a much easier way than that by which I went up. Later I returned several times, and from a distance watched the eaglets being fed. But I never climbed to the nest again.

One day, when I came to the little thicket on the cliff where I used to lie and watch the nest through my glass, I found that one eaglet was gone. The other stood on the edge of the nest, looking down fearfully into the abyss, whither, no doubt, his bolder nest mate had flown, and calling disconsolately from time to time. His whole attitude showed plainly that he was hungry and cross and lonesome. Presently the mother-eagle came swiftly up from the valley, and there was food in her talons. She came to the edge of the nest, hovered over it a moment, so as to give the hungry eaglet a sight and smell of food, then went slowly down to the valley, taking the food with her, telling the little one in her own way to come and he should have it. He called after her loudly from the edge of the nest, and spread his wings a dozen times to follow. But the plunge was too awful; his heart failed him; and he settled back in the nest, and pulled his head down into his shoulders, and shut his eyes, and tried to forget that he was hungry. The meaning of the little comedy was plain enough. She was trying to teach him to fly, telling him that his wings were grown and the time was come to use them; but he was afraid.

In a little while she came back again, this time without food, and hovered over the nest, trying every way to induce the little one to leave it. She succeeded at last, when with a desperate effort he sprang upward and flapped to the ledge above, where I had sat and watched him with Old Whitehead. Then, after surveying the world gravely from his new place, he flapped back to the nest, and turned a deaf ear to all his mother's assurances that he could fly just as easily to the tree-tops below, if he only would.

Suddenly, as if discouraged, she rose well above him. I held my breath, for I knew what was coming. The little fellow stood on the edge of the nest, looking down at the plunge which he dared not take. There was a sharp cry from behind, which made him alert, tense as a watch-spring. The next instant the mother-eagle had swooped, striking the nest at his feet, sending his support of twigs and himself with them out into the air together.

He was afloat now, afloat on the blue air in spite of himself, and flapped lustily for life. Over him, under him, beside him hovered the mother on tireless wings, calling softly that she was there. But the awful fear of the depths and the lance tops of the spruces was upon the little one; his flapping grew more wild; he fell faster and faster. Suddenly — more in fright, it seemed to me, than because he had spent his strength — he lost his balance and tipped head downward in the air. It was all over now, it seemed; he folded his wings to be dashed in pieces among the trees. Then like a flash the old mother-eagle shot under him; his despairing feet touched her broad shoulders, between her wings. He righted himself, rested an instant, found his head; then she dropped like a shot from under him, leaving him to come down on his own wings. A handful of feathers, torn out by his claws, hovered slowly down after them.

It was all the work of an instant before I lost them among the trees far below. And when I found them again with my glass, the eaglet was in the top of a great pine, and the mother was feeding him.

And then, standing there alone in the great wilderness, it flashed upon me for the first time just what the wise old prophet meant; though he wrote long ago, in a distant land, and another than Cloud Wings had taught her little ones, all unconscious of the kindly eyes that watched out of a thicket: "As the eagle stirreth up her nest, fluttereth over her young, spreadeth abroad her wings, taketh them, beareth them on her wings, — so the Lord."

VII. UPWEEKIS THE SHADOW.

"LONG 'go, O long time 'go," so says Simmo the Indian, Upweekis the lynx came to Clote Scarpe one day with a complaint. "See," he said, "you are good to everybody but me. Pekquam the fisher is cunning and patient; he can catch what he will. Lhoks the panther is strong and tireless; nothing can get away from him, not even the great moose. And Mooween the bear sleeps all winter, when game is scarce, and in summer eats everything,—roots and mice and berries and dead fish and meat and honey and red ants. So he is always full and happy. But my eyes are no good; they are bright, like Cheplahgan the eagle's, yet they cannot see anything unless it moves; for you have made every creature that hides just like the place he hides in. My nose is worse; it cannot smell

Seksagadagee the grouse, though I walk over him asleep in the snow. And my feet make a noise in the leaves, so that Moktaques the rabbit hears me, and hides, and laughs behind me when I go to catch him. And I am always hungry. Make me now like the shadows that play, in order that nothing may notice me when I go hunting."

So Clote Scarpe, the great chief who was kind to all animals, gave Upweekis a soft gray coat that is almost invisible in the woods, summer or winter, and made his feet large, and padded them with soft fur; so that indeed he is like the shadows that play, for you can neither see nor hear him. But Clote Scarpe remembered Moktaques the rabbit also, and gave him two coats, a brown one for summer and a white one for winter. Consequently he is harder than ever to see when he is quiet; and Upweekis must still depend upon his wits to catch him. As Upweekis has few wits to spare, Moktaques often sees him close at hand, and chuckles in his form under the brown ferns, or sits up straight under the snow-covered hemlock tips, and watches the big lynx at his hunting.

Sometimes, on a winter night, when you camp in the wilderness, and the snow is sifting down into your fire, and the woods are all still, a fierce screech breaks suddenly out of the darkness just behind your windbreak of boughs. You jump to your feet and grab your rifle; but Simmo, who is down on his knees before the fire frying pork, only turns his head to listen a moment, and says: "Upweekis catch-um rabbit dat time." Then he gets closer to the fire, for the screech was not pleasant, and goes on with his cooking.

You are more curious than he, or you want the big cat's skin to take home with you. You steal away towards the cry, past the little *commoosie*, or shelter, that you made hastily at sundown when the trail ended. There, with your back to the fire and the *commoosie* between, the light does not dazzle your eyes; you can trace the shadows creeping in and out stealthily among the underbrush. But if Upweekis is there — and he probably is — you do not see him. He is a shadow among the shadows. Only there is this difference: shadows move no bushes. As you watch, a fir-tip stirs; a bit of snow drops down. You gaze intently at the spot. Then out of the deep shadow two living coals are suddenly kindled. They grow larger and larger, glowing, flashing, burning holes into your eyes till you brush them swiftly with your hand. A shiver runs over you, for to look into the eyes of a lynx at night, when the light catches them, is a scary experience. Your rifle jumps to position; the glowing coals are quenched on the instant. Then, when your eyes have blinked the fascination out of them, the shadows go creeping in and out again, and Upweekis is lost amongst them.

Sometimes, indeed, you see him again. Moktaques, the big white hare, who forgets a thing the moment it is past, sees you standing there and is full of curiosity. He forgets that he was being hunted a moment ago, and comes hopping along to see what you are. You back away toward the fire. He scampers off in a fright, but presently comes hopping after you. Watch the underbrush behind him sharply. In a moment it stirs stealthily, as if a shadow were moving it; and there is the lynx, stealing along in the snow with his eyes blazing. Again Moktaques feels that he is hunted, and does the only safe thing; he crouches low in the snow, where a fir-tip bends over him, and is still as the earth. His color hides him perfectly.

Upweekis has lost the trail again; he wavers back and forth, like a shadow under a swinging lamp, turning his great head from side to side. He cannot see nor hear nor smell his game; but he saw a bit of snow fly a moment ago, and knows that it came from Moktaques' big pads. Don't stir now; be still as the great spruce in whose shadow you stand; and, once in a hunter's lifetime perhaps, you will see a curious tragedy.

The lynx settles himself in the snow, with all four feet close together, ready for a spring. As you watch and wonder, a screech rings out through the woods, so sharp and fierce that no rabbit's nerves can stand it close at hand and be still. Moktaques jumps straight up in the air. The lynx sees it, whirls, hurls himself at the spot. Another screech, a different one, and then you know that it's all over.

And that is why Upweekis' cry is so fierce and sudden on a winter night. Your fire attracts the rabbits. Upweekis knows this, or is perhaps attracted himself and comes also, and hides among the shadows. But he never catches anything unless he blunders onto it. That is why he wanders so much in winter and passes twenty rabbits before he catches one. So when he knows that Moktaques is near, watching the light, but remaining himself invisible, Upweekis crouches for a spring; then he screeches fearfully. Moktaques hears it and is startled, as anybody else would be, hearing such a cry near him. He jumps in a fright and pays the penalty.

If the lynx is a big one, and very hungry, as he generally is in winter, you may get some unpleasant impressions of him in another way when you venture

Upweekis the Shadow.

far from your fire. His eyes blaze out at you from the darkness, just two big glowing spots, which are all you see, and which disappear at your first motion. Then as you strain your eyes, and watch and listen, you feel the coals upon you again from another place; and there they are, under a bush on your left, creeping closer and blazing deep red. They disappear suddenly as the lynx turns his head, only to reappear and fascinate you from another point. So he plays with you as if you were a great mouse, creeping closer all the time, swishing his stub tail fiercely to lash himself up to the courage point of springing. But his movements are so still and shadowy that unless he follows you as you back away to the fire, and so comes within the circle of light, the chances are that you will never see him.

Indeed the chances are always that way, day or night, unless you turn hunter and set a trap for him in the rabbit paths which he follows nightly, and hang a bait over it to make him look up and forget his steps. In summer he goes to the burned lands for the rabbits that swarm in the thickets, and to rear his young in seclusion. You find his tracks there all about, and the marks of his killing; but though you watch and prowl all day and come home in the twilight, you will learn little. He hears you and skulks away amid the lights and shadows of the hillside, and so hides himself — in plain sight, sometimes, like a young partridge — that he manages to keep a clean record in the notebook where you hoped to write down all about him.

In winter you cross his tracks, great round tracks that wander everywhere through the big woods, and you think: Now I shall find him surely. But though you follow for miles and learn much about him, finding where he passed this rabbit close at hand, without suspecting it, and caught that one by accident, and missed the partridge that burst out of the snow under his very feet, — still Upweekis himself remains only a shadow of the woods. Once, after a glorious long tramp on his trail, I found the spot where he had been sleeping a moment before. But beside that experience I must put fifty other trails that I have followed, of which I never saw the end nor the beginning. And whenever I have found out anything about Upweekis it has generally come unexpectedly, as most good things do.

Once the chance came as I was watching a muskrat at his supper. It was twilight in the woods. I had drifted in close to shore in my canoe to see what Musquash was doing on top of a rock. All muskrats have favorite eating places — a rock, a stranded log, a tree boll that leans out over the water, and always a

Upweekis the Shadow. 115

pretty spot — whither they bring food from a distance, evidently for the purpose of eating it where they feel most at home. This one had gathered a half dozen big fresh-water clams onto his dining table, and sat down in the midst to enjoy the feast. He would take a clam in his fore paws, whack it a few times on the rock till the shell cracked, then open it with his teeth and devour the morsel inside. He ate leisurely, tasting each clam critically before swallowing, and sitting up often to wash his whiskers or to look out over the lake. A hermit thrush sang marvelously sweet above him; the twilight colors glowed deep and deeper in the water below, where his shadow was clearly eating clams also, in the midst of heaven's splendor.— Altogether a pretty scene, and a moment of peace that I still love to remember. I quite forgot that Musquash is a villain. But the tragedy was near, as it always is in the wilderness. Suddenly a movement caught my eye on the bank above. Something was waving nervously under the bushes. Before I could make out what it was, there was a fearful rush, a gleam of wild yellow eyes, a squeak from the muskrat. Then Upweekis, looking gaunt and dark and strange in his summer coat, was crouched on the rock with Musquash between his great paws, growling fiercely as he cracked the bones. He bit his game all over, to make sure that it was quite dead, then took it by the back of the neck, glided into the bushes with his stub tail twitching, and became a shadow again.

Another time I was perched up in a lodged tree, some twenty feet from the ground, watching a big bait of fish which I had put in an open spot for anything that might choose to come and get it. I was hoping for a bear, and so climbed above the ground that he might not get my scent should he come from leeward. It was early autumn, and my intentions were wholly peaceable. I had no weapon of any kind.

Late in the afternoon something took to chasing a red squirrel near me. I heard them scurrying through the trees, but could see nothing. The chase passed out of hearing, and I had almost forgotten it, for something was moving in the underbrush near my bait, when back it came with a rush. The squirrel, half dead with fright, leaped from a spruce-tip to the ground, jumped onto the tree in which I sat, and raced up the incline, almost to my feet, where he sprang to a branch and sat chattering hysterically between two fears. After him came a pine marten, following swiftly, catching the scent of his game, not from the bark or the ground, but apparently from the air. Scarcely had he jumped upon my tree when there was a screech and a rush in the underbrush just below him, and out of the bushes came a young lynx to join in the chase. He missed the marten on the ground, but sprang to my tree like a flash. I remember still that the only sound I was conscious of at the time was the ripping of his nails in the dead bark. He had been seeking my bait undoubtedly—for it was a good lynx country, and Upweekis loves fish like a cat—when the chase passed under his nose and he joined it on the instant.

Halfway up the incline the marten smelled me, or was terrified by the noise behind him and leaped aside. A branch upon which I was leaning swayed or snapped, and the lucivee stopped as if struck, crouching lower and lower against the tree, his big yellow expressionless eyes glaring straight into mine. A moment only he stood the steady look; then his eyes wavered; he turned his head, leaped for the underbrush, and was gone.

Another moment and Meeko the squirrel had forgotten his fright and peril and everything else save his curiosity to find out who I was and all about me. He had to pass quite close to me to get to another tree, but anything was better than going back where the marten might be waiting; so he was presently over my head, snickering and barking to make me move, and scolding me soundly for disturbing the peace of the woods.

In summer Upweekis is a solitary creature, rearing his young away back on the wildest burned lands, where game is plenty and where it is almost impossible to find him except by accident. In winter also he roams alone for the most part; but occasionally, when rabbits are scarce, as they are periodically in the northern woods, he gathers in small bands for the purpose of pulling down big game that he would never attack singly. Generally Upweekis is skulking and cowardly with man; but when driven by hunger (as I found out once) or when hunting in bands, he is a savage beast and must be followed cautiously.

I had heard much of the fierceness of these hunting bands from settlers and hunters; and once a friend of mine, an old backwoodsman, had a narrow escape from them. He had a dog, Grip, a big brindled cur, of whose prowess in killing "varmints" he was always bragging, calling him the best "lucififer" dog in all Canada. Lucififer, by the way, is a local name for the lynx on the upper St. John, where Grip and his master lived.

One day in winter the master missed a young heifer and went on his trail, with Grip and his axe for companions. Presently he came to lynx tracks, then to signs of a struggle, then plump upon six or seven of the big cats snarling savagely over the body of the heifer. Grip, the lucififer dog, rushed in blindly, and in two minutes was torn to ribbons. Then the lynxes came creeping and snarling towards the man, who backed away, shouting and swinging his axe. He killed one by a lucky blow, as it sprang for his chest. The others drove him to his own door; but he would never have reached it, so he told me, but for a long strip of open land that he had cleared back into the woods. He would face and charge the beasts, which seemed more afraid of his voice than of the axe, then run desperately to keep them from circling and getting between him and safety. When he reached the open strip they followed a little way along the edges of the underbrush, but returned one at a time when they were sure he had no further mind to disturb their feast or their fighting.

It is curious that when Upweekis and his hunting pack pull down game in this way the first thing they do is to fight over it. There may be meat enough and to spare, but under their fearful hunger is the old beastly instinct for each one to grab all for himself; so they fall promptly to teeth and claws before the game is dead. The fightings at such times are savage affairs, both to the eye and ear. One forgets that Upweekis is a shadow, and thinks that he must be a fiend.

One day in winter, when after caribou, I came upon a very large lynx track, the largest I have ever seen. It was two days old; but it led in my direction, toward the caribou barrens, and I followed it to see what I should see.

Presently it joined four other lynx trails, and a mile farther on all five trails went forward in great flying leaps, each lynx leaving a hole in the snow as big as a bucket at every jump. A hundred yards of this kind of traveling and the trails joined another trail,—that of a wounded caribou from the barrens. His tracks showed that he had been traveling with difficulty on three legs. Here was a place where he had stood to listen; and there was another place where even untrained eyes might see that he had plunged forward with a start of fear. It was a silent story, but full of eager interest in every detail.

The lucivee tracks now showed different tactics. They crossed and crisscrossed the trail, appearing now in front, now behind, now on either side the wounded bull, evidently closing in upon him warily. Here and there was a depression in the snow where one had crouched, growling, as the game passed. Then the struggle began. First, there was a trampled place in the snow where the bull had taken a stand and the big cats went creeping about him, waiting for a chance to

The stripped carcass of the caribou with two lynxes still upon it

spring all together. He broke away from that, but the three-legged gallop speedily exhausted him. Only when he trots is a caribou tireless. The lynxes followed; the deadly cat-play began again. First one, then another leaped, only to be shaken off; then two, then all five were upon the poor brute, which still struggled forward. The record was written red all over the snow.

As I followed it cautiously, a snarl sounded just ahead. I kicked off my snowshoes and circled noiselessly to the left, so as to look out over a little opening. There lay the stripped carcass of the caribou with two lynxes still upon it, growling fearfully at each other as they pulled at the bones. Another lynx crouched in the snow, under a bush, watching the scene. Two others circled about each other snarling, looking for an opening, but too well fed to care for a fight just then. Two or three foxes, a pine marten, and a fisher moved ceaselessly in and out, sniffing hungrily, and waiting for a chance to seize every scrap of bone or skin that was left unguarded for an instant. Above them a dozen moose birds kept the same watch vigilantly. As I stole nearer, hoping to get behind an old log where I could lie and watch the spectacle, some creature scurried out of the underbrush at one side. I was watching the movement, when a loud *kee-yaaah!* startled me; I whirled towards the opening. From behind the old log a fierce round head with tasseled ears rose up, and the big lynx, whose trail I had first followed, sprang into sight snarling and spitting viciously.

The feast stopped at the first alarm. The marten disappeared instantly. The foxes and the fisher and one lynx slunk away. Another, which I had not seen, stalked up to the carcass and put his fore paws upon it, and turned his savage head in my direction. Evidently other lynxes had come in to the kill beside the five I had followed. Then all the big cats crouched in the snow and stared at me steadily out of their wild yellow eyes.

It was only for a moment. The big lynx on my side of the log was in a fighting temper; he snarled continuously. Another sprang over the log and crouched beside him, facing me. Then began a curious scene, of which I could not wait to see the end. The two lynxes hitched nearer and nearer to where I stood motionless, watching. They would creep forward a step or two, then crouch in the snow, like a cat warming her feet, and stare at me unblinkingly for a few moments. Then another hitch or two, which brought them nearer, and another stare. I could not look at one steadily, to make him waver; for the moment my eyes were upon him the others hitched closer; and already two more lynxes were coming over the log. I had to draw the curtain hastily with a bullet between the yellow eyes of the biggest lynx, and a second straight into the chest of his fellow-starer, just as he wriggled down into the snow for a spring. The others had leaped away snarling as the first heavy report rolled through the woods.

Another time, in the same region, a solitary lynx made me uncomfortable for half an afternoon. It was Sunday, and I had gone for a snowshoe tramp, leaving my rifle behind me. On the way back to camp I stopped for a caribou head and skin, which I had *cached* on the edge of a barren the morning before. The weather had changed; a bitter cold wind blew after me as I turned toward camp. I carried the head with its branching antlers on my shoulder; the skin hung down, to keep my back warm, its edges trailing in the snow.

Gradually I became convinced that something was following me; but I turned several times without seeing anything. "It is only a fisher," I thought, and kept on steadily, instead of going back to examine my trail; for I was hoping for a glimpse of the cunning creature whose trail you find so often running side by side with your own, and who follows you, if you have any trace of game about you, hour after hour through the wilderness, without ever showing himself in the light. Then I whirled suddenly, obeying an impulse; and there was Upweekis, a big, savage-looking fellow, just gliding up on my trail in plain sight, following the broad snowshoe track and the scent of the fresh caribou skin without difficulty, poor trailer though he be.

He stopped and sat down on his feet, as a lucivee generally does when you surprise him, and stared at me steadily. When I went on again I knew that he was after me, though he had disappeared from the trail.

Then began a double-quick of four miles, the object being to reach camp before night should fall and give the lucivee the advantage. It was already late enough to make one a bit uneasy. He knew that I was hurrying; he grew bolder, showing himself openly on the trail behind me. I turned into an old swamping road, which gave me a bit of open before and behind. Then I saw him occasionally on either side, or crouching half hid until I passed. Clearly he was waiting for night; but to this day I am not sure whether it was the man or the caribou skin upon which he had set his heart. The scent of flesh and blood was in his nose, and he was too hungry to control himself much longer.

Upweekis the Shadow.

I cut a good club with my big jack-knife, and, watching my chance, threw off the caribou head and jumped for him as he crouched in the snow. He leaped aside untouched, but crouched again instantly, showing all his teeth, snarling horribly. Three times I swung at him warily. Each time he jumped aside and watched for his opening; but I kept the club in play before his eyes, and it was not yet dark enough. Then I yelled in his face, to teach him fear, and went on again.

Near camp I shouted for Simmo to bring my rifle; but he was slow in understanding, and his answering shout alarmed the savage creature near me. His movements became instantly more wary, more hidden. He left the open trail; and once, when I saw him well behind me, his head was raised high, listening. I threw down the caribou head to keep him busy, and ran for camp. In a few minutes I was stealing back again with my rifle; but Upweekis had felt the change in the situation and was again among the shadows, where he belongs. I lost his trail in the darkening woods.

There was another lynx which showed me, one day, a different side to Upweekis' nature. It was in summer, when every creature in the wilderness seems an altogether different creature from the one you knew last winter, with new habits, new duties, new pleasures, and even a new coat to hide him better from his enemies.

Opposite my island camp, where I halted a little while in a summer's roving, was a burned ridge; that is, it had been burned over years before; now it was a perfect tangle, with many an open sunny spot, however, where berries grew by handfuls. Rabbits swarmed there, and grouse were plenty. As it was forty miles back from the settlements, it seemed a perfect place for Upweekis to make a den in. And so it was. I have no doubt there were a dozen litters of kittens on that two miles of ridge; but the cover was so dense that nothing smaller than a deer could be seen moving.

For two weeks I hunted the ridge whenever I was not fishing, stealing in and out among the thickets, depending more upon ears than eyes, but seeing nothing of Upweekis, save here and there a trampled fern, or a blood-splashed leaf, with a bit of rabbit fur, or a great round cat track, to tell the story. Once I came upon a bear and two cubs among the berries; and once, when the wind was blowing down the hill, I walked almost up to a bull caribou without seeing him. He was watching my approach curiously, only his eyes, ears, and horns showing above the tangle where he stood. Down in the coverts it was always intensely still, with a stillness that I took good care not to break. So when the great brute whirled with a snort and a tremendous crash of bushes, almost under my nose, it raised my hair for a moment, not knowing what the creature was, nor which way he was heading. But though every day brought its experience, and its knowledge, and its new wonder at the ways of wild things, I found no trace of the den, nor of the kittens I had hoped to watch. All animals are silent near their little ones, so there was never a cry by night or day to guide me.

Late one afternoon, when I had climbed to the top of the ridge and was on my way back to camp, I ran into an odor, the strong, disagreeable odor that always hovers about the den of a carnivorous animal. I followed it through a thicket, and came to an open stony place, with a sharp drop of five or six feet to dense cover below. The odor came from this cover, so I jumped down; when — *yeow, karrrr, pft-pft!* Almost under my feet a gray thing leaped away snarling, followed by another. I had the merest glimpse of them; but from the way they bristled and spit and arched their backs, I knew that I had stumbled upon a pair of the lynx kittens, for which I had searched so long in vain.

They had, probably, been lying out on the warm stones, until, hearing strange footsteps, they had glided away to cover. When I crashed down near them they had been scared into showing their temper; else I had never seen them in the underbrush. Fortunately for me, the fierce old mother was away. Had she been there, I should undoubtedly have had more serious business on hand than watching her kittens.

They had not seen more of me than my shoes and stockings; so when I stole after them, to see what they were like, they were waiting under a bush to see what I was like. They jumped away again, spitting, without seeing me, alarmed by the rustle which I could not avoid making in the cover. So I followed them, just a quiver of leaves here, a snarl there, and then a rush away, until they doubled back towards the rocky place, where, parting the underbrush cautiously, I saw a dark hole among the rocks of a little opening. The roots of an upturned tree arched over the hole, making a broad doorway. In this doorway stood two half-grown lucivees, fuzzy and gray and savage-looking, their backs still up, their wild eyes turned in my direction apprehensively. Seeing me they drew farther back into the den, and I saw nothing more of them save now and then their round heads, or the fire in their yellow eyes.

It was too late for further observation that day. The fierce old mother lynx would presently be back; they would let her know of the intruder in some way;

and they would all keep close in the den. I found a place, some dozen yards above, where it would be possible to watch them, marked the spot by a blasted stub, to which I made a compass of broken twigs; and then went back to camp.

Next morning I omitted the early fishing, and was back at the place before the sun looked over the ridge. Their den was all quiet, in deep shadow. Mother Lynx was still away on the early hunting. I intended to kill her when she came back. My rifle lay ready across my knees. Then I would watch the kittens a little while, and kill them also. I wanted their skins, all soft and fine with their first fur. And they were too big and fierce to think of taking them alive. My vacation was over. Simmo was already packing up, to break camp that morning. So there would be no time to carry out my long-cherished plan of watching young lynxes at play, as I had before watched young foxes and bears and owls and fish-hawks, and indeed almost everything, except Upweekis, in the wilderness.

Presently one of the lucivees came out, yawned, stretched, raised himself against a root. In the morning stillness I could hear the cut and rip of his claws on the wood. We call the action sharpening the claws; but it is only the occasional exercise of the fine flexor muscles that a cat uses so seldom, yet must use powerfully when the time comes. The second lucivee came out of the shadow a moment later and leaped upon the fallen tree where he could better watch the hillside below. For half an hour or more, while I waited expectantly, both animals moved restlessly about the den, or climbed over the roots and trunk of the fallen tree. They were plainly cross; they made no attempt at play, but kept well away from each other with a wholesome respect for teeth and claws and temper. Breakfast hour was long past, evidently, and they were hungry.

Suddenly one, who was at that moment watching from the tree trunk, leaped down; the second joined him, and both paced back and forth excitedly. They had heard the sounds of a coming that were too fine for my ears. A stir in the underbrush, and Mother Lynx, a great savage creature, stalked out proudly. She carried a dead hare gripped across the middle of the back. The long ears on one side, the long legs on the other, hung limply, showing a fresh kill. She walked to the doorway of her den, crossed it back and forth two or three times, still carrying the hare as if the lust of blood were raging within her and she could not drop her prey even to her own little ones, which followed her hungrily, one on either side. Once, as she turned toward me, one of the kittens seized a leg of the hare

Upweekis the Shadow.

and jerked it savagely. The mother whirled on him, growling deep down in her throat; the youngster backed away, scared but snarling. At last she flung the game down. The kittens fell upon it like furies, growling at each other, as I had seen the stranger lynxes growling once before over the caribou. In a moment they had torn the carcass apart and were crouched, each one over his piece, gnarling like a cat over a rat, and stuffing themselves greedily in utter forgetfulness of the mother lynx, which lay under a bush some distance away and watched them.

In a half hour the savage meal was over. The little ones sat up, licked their chops, and began to tongue their broad paws. The mother had been blinking sleepily; now she rose and came to her young. A change had come over the family. The kittens ran to meet the dam as if they had not seen her before, rubbing softly against her legs, or sitting up to rub their whiskers against hers — a tardy thanks for the breakfast she had provided. The fierce old mother too seemed altogether different. She arched her back against the roots, purring loudly, while the little ones arched and purred against her sides. Then she bent her savage head and licked them fondly with her tongue, while they rubbed as close to her as they could get, passing between her legs as under a bridge, and trying to lick her face in return; till all their tongues were going at once and the family lay down together.

It was time to kill them now. The rifle lay ready. But a change had come over the watcher too. Hitherto he had seen Upweekis as a ferocious brute, whom it was good to kill. This was altogether different. Upweekis could be gentle also, it seemed, and give herself for her little ones. And a bit of tenderness, like that which lay so unconscious under my eyes, gets hold of a man, and spikes his guns better than moralizing. So the watcher stole away, making as little noise as he could, following his compass of twigs to where the canoes lay ready and Simmo was waiting.

Sometime, I hope, Simmo and I will camp there again, in winter. And then I shall listen with a new interest for a cry in the night which tells me that Moktaques the rabbit is hiding close at hand in the snow, where a young lynx of my acquaintance cannot find him.

VIII. HUKWEEM THE NIGHT VOICE.

HUKWEEM the loon must go through the world crying for what he never gets, and searching for one whom he never finds; for he is the hunting-dog of Clote Scarpe. So said Simmo to me one night in explaining why the loon's cry is so wild and sad.

Clote Scarpe, by the way, is the legendary hero, the Hiawatha of the northern Indians. Long ago he lived on the Wollastook, and ruled the animals, which all lived peaceably together, understanding each other's language, and "nobody ever ate anybody," as Simmo says. But when Clote Scarpe went away they quarreled, and Lhoks the panther and Nemox the fisher took to killing the other animals. Malsun the wolf soon followed, and ate all he killed; and Meeko the squirrel, who always makes all the mischief he can, set even the peaceable animals by the ears, so that they feared and distrusted each other.

Then they scattered through the big woods, living each one for himself; and now the strong ones kill the weak, and nobody understands anybody any more.

There were no dogs in those days. Hukweem was Clote Scarpe's hunting companion when he hunted the great evil beasts that disturbed the wilderness; and Hukweem alone, of all the birds and animals, remained true to his master. For hunting makes strong friendship, says Simmo; and that is true. Therefore does Hukweem go through the world, looking for his master and calling him to come back. Over the tree-tops, when he flies low looking for new waters; high in air, out of sight, on his southern migrations; and on every lake where he is only a voice, the sad night voice of the vast solitary unknown wilderness—everywhere you hear him seeking. Even on the seacoast in winter, where he knows Clote Scarpe cannot be — for Clote Scarpe hates the sea — Hukweem forgets himself, and cries occasionally out of pure loneliness.

When I asked what Hukweem says when he cries — for all cries of the wilderness have their interpretation — Simmo answered: "Wy, he say two ting. First he say, *Where are you? O where are you?* Dass what you call-um his laugh, like he crazy. Denn, wen nobody answer, he say, *O I so sorry, so sorry!*

Hukweem's curiosity could stand it no longer

Ooooo-eee! like woman lost in woods. An' dass his tother cry."

This comes nearer to explaining the wild unearthliness of Hukweem's call than anything else I know. It makes things much simpler to understand, when you are camped deep in the wilderness, and the night falls, and out of the misty darkness under the farther shore comes a wild shivering call that makes one's nerves tingle till he finds out about it — *Where are you? O where are you?* That is just like Hukweem.

Sometimes, however, he varies the cry, and asks very plainly: "Who are you? O who are you?" There was a loon on the Big Squattuk lake, where I camped one summer, which was full of inquisitiveness as a blue jay. He lived alone at one end of the lake, while his mate, with her brood of two, lived at the other end, nine miles away. Every morning and evening he came close to my camp — very much nearer than is usual, for loons are wild and shy in the wilderness — to cry out his challenge. Once, late at night, I flashed a lantern at the end of the old log that served as a landing for the canoes, where I had heard strange ripples; and there was Hukweem, examining everything with the greatest curiosity.

Every unusual thing in our doings made him inquisitive to know all about it. Once, when I started down the lake with a fair wind, and a small spruce set up in the bow of my canoe for a sail, he followed me four or five miles, calling all the way. And when I came back to camp at twilight with a big bear in the canoe, his shaggy head showing over the bow, and his legs up over the middle thwart, like a little old black man with his wrinkled feet on the table, Hukweem's curiosity could stand it no longer. He swam up within twenty yards, and circled the canoe half a dozen times, sitting up straight on his tail by a vigorous use of his wings, stretching his neck like an inquisitive duck, so as to look into the canoe and see what queer thing I had brought with me.

He had another curious habit which afforded him unending amusement. There was a deep bay on the west shore of the lake, with hills rising abruptly on three sides. The echo here was remarkable; a single shout brought a dozen distinct answers, and then a confusion of tongues as the echoes and re-echoes from many hills met and mingled. I discovered the place in an interesting way.

One evening at twilight, as I was returning to camp from exploring the upper lake, I heard a wild crying of loons on the west side. There seemed to be five or six of the great divers, all laughing and shrieking like so many lunatics. Pushing over to investigate, I noticed for the first time the entrance to a great bay, and paddled up cautiously behind a point, so as to surprise the loons at their game. For they play games, just as crows do. But when I looked in, there was only one bird, Hukweem the Inquisitive. I knew him instantly by his great size and beautiful markings. He would give a single sharp call, and listen intently, with head up, swinging from side to side as the separate echoes came ringing back from the hills. Then he would try his cackling laugh, *Ooo-áh-ha-ha-ha-hoo, ooo-áh-ha-ha-ha-hoo*, and as the echoes began to ring about his head he would get excited, sitting up on his tail, flapping his wings, cackling and shrieking with glee at his own performance. Every wild syllable was flung back like a shot from the surrounding hills, till the air seemed full of loons, all mingling their crazy cachinnations with the din of the chief performer. The uproar made one shiver. Then Hukweem would cease suddenly, listening intently to the warring echoes. Before the confusion was half ended he would get excited again, and swim about in small circles, spreading wings and tail, showing his fine feathers as if every echo were an admiring loon, pleased as a peacock with himself at having made such a noise in a quiet world.

There was another loon, a mother bird, on a different lake, whose two eggs had been carried off by a thieving muskrat; but she did not know who did it, for Musquash knows how to roll the eggs into water and carry them off, before eating, where the mother bird will not find the shells. She came swimming down to meet us the moment our canoe entered the lake; and what she seemed to cry was, "Where are they? O where are they?" She followed us across the lake, accusing us of robbery, and asking the same question over and over.

But whatever the meaning of Hukweem's crying, it seems to constitute a large part of his existence. Indeed, it is as a cry that he is chiefly known — the wild, unearthly cry of the wilderness night. His education for this begins very early. Once I was exploring the grassy shores of a wild lake when a mother loon appeared suddenly, out in the middle, with a great splashing and crying. I paddled out to see what was the matter. She withdrew with a great effort, apparently, as I approached, still crying loudly and beating the water with her wings. "Oho," I said, "you have a nest in there somewhere, and now you are trying to get me away from it." This was the only time I have ever known a loon to try that old mother bird's trick. Generally they slip off the nest while the canoe is yet half a mile away, and swim under water a long distance, and watch you silently from the other side of the lake.

I went back and hunted awhile for the nest among the bogs of a little bay; then left the search to investigate a strange call that sounded continuously farther up the shore. It came from some hidden spot in the tall grass, an eager little whistling cry, reminding me somehow of a nest of young fish-hawks.

As I waded cautiously among the bogs, trying to locate the sound, I came suddenly upon the loon's nest — just the bare top of a bog, where the mother bird had pulled up the grass and hollowed the earth enough to keep the eggs from rolling out. They were there on the bare ground, two very large olive eggs with dark blotches. I left them undisturbed and went on to investigate the crying, which had stopped a moment as I approached the nest.

Presently it began again behind me, faint at first, then louder and more eager, till I traced it back to Hukweem's household. But there was nothing here to account for it, only two innocent-looking eggs on top of a bog. I bent over to examine them more closely. There, on the sides, were two holes, and out of the holes projected the points of two tiny bills. Inside were two little loons, crying at the top of their lungs, "Let me out! O let me out! It's hot in here. Let me out — *Oooo-eee! pip-pip-pip!*"

But I left the work of release to the mother bird,

thinking she knew more about it. Next day I went back to the place, and, after much watching, saw two little loons stealing in and out among the bogs, exulting in their freedom, but silent as two shadows. The mother bird was off on the lake, fishing for their dinner.

Hukweem's fishing is always an interesting thing to watch. Unfortunately he is so shy that one seldom gets a good opportunity. Once I found his favorite fishing ground, and came every day to watch him from a thicket on the shore. It was of little use to go in a canoe. At my approach he would sink deeper and deeper in the water, as if taking in ballast. How he does this is a mystery; for his body is much lighter than its bulk of water. Dead or alive, it floats like a cork; yet without any perceptible motion, by an effort of will apparently, he sinks it out of sight. You are approaching in your canoe, and he moves off slowly, swinging his head from side to side so as to look at you first with one eye, then with the other. Your canoe is swift; he sees that you are gaining, that you are already too near. He swings on the water, and sits watching you steadily. Suddenly he begins to sink, deeper and deeper, till his back is just awash. Go a little nearer, and now his body disappears; only his neck and head remain above water. Raise your hand, or make any quick motion, and he is gone altogether. He dives like a flash, swims deep and far, and when he comes to the surface will be well out of danger.

If you notice the direction of his bill as it enters the water, you can tell fairly well about where he will come up again. It was confusing at first, in chasing him, to find that he rarely came up where he was expected. I would paddle hard in the direction he was going, only to find him far to the right or left, or behind me, when at last he showed himself. That was because I followed his body, not his bill. Moving in one direction, he will turn his head and dive. That is to mislead you, if you are following him. Follow his bill, as he does himself, and you will be near him when he rises; for he rarely turns under water.

With two good men to paddle, it is not difficult to tire him out. Though he swims with extraordinary rapidity under water — fast enough to follow and catch a trout — a long deep dive tires him, and he must rest before another. If you are chasing him, shout and wave your hat the moment he appears, and paddle hard the way his bill points as he dives again. The next time he comes up you are nearer to him. Send him down again quick, and after him. The next time he is frightened to see the canoe so close, and dives deep, which tires him the more. So his disappearances become shorter and more confused; you follow him more surely because you can see him plainly now as he goes down. Suddenly he bursts out of water beside you, scattering the spray into your canoe. Once he came up under my paddle, and I plucked a feather from his back before he got away.

This last appearance always scares him out of his wits, and you get what you have been working hard for—a sight of Hukweem getting under way. Away he goes in a smother of spray, beating the water with his wings, kicking hard to lift himself up; and so for a hundred yards, leaving a wake like a stern-wheel steamer, till he gathers headway enough to rise from the water.

After that first start there is no sign of awkwardness. His short wings rise and fall with a rapidity that tries the eye to follow, like the rush of a coot down wind to decoys. You can hear the swift, strong beat of them, far over your head, when he is not calling. His flight is very rapid, very even, and often at enormous altitudes. But when he wants to come down he always gets frightened, thinking of his short wings, and how high he is, and how fast he is going. On the ocean, in winter, where he has all the room he wants, he sometimes comes down in a great incline, miles long, and plunges through and over a dozen

Hukweem the Night Voice. 143

waves, like a dolphin, before he can stop. But where the lake is small, and he cannot come down that way, he has a dizzy time of it.

Once, on a little lake in September, I used to watch for hours to get a sight of the process. Twelve or fifteen loons were gathered there, holding high carnival. They called down every migrating loon that passed that way; their numbers increased daily. Twilight was the favorite time for arriving. In the stillness I would hear Hukweem far away, so high that he was only a voice. Presently I would see him whirling over the lake in a great circle.— " Come down, O come down," cry all the loons. " I 'm afraid, *ooo-ho-ho-ho-ho-hoooo-eee*, I 'm afraid," says Hukweem, who is perhaps a little loon, all the way from Labrador on his first migration, and has never come down from a height before. " Come on, O come *oh-ho-ho-ho-ho-hon*. It won't hurt you; we did it; come on," cry all the loons.

Then Hukweem would slide lower with each circle, whirling round and round the lake in a great spiral, yelling all the time, and all the loons answering. When low enough, he would set his wings and plunge like a catapult at the very midst of the assembly, which scattered wildly, yelling like schoolboys — " Look out! he 'll break his neck; he 'll hit you; he'll break your back if he hits you."—So they splashed away in a desperate fright, each one looking back over his shoulder to see Hukweem come down, which he would do at a terrific pace, striking the water with a mighty splash, and shooting half across the lake in a smother of white, before he could get his legs under him and turn around. Then all the loons would gather round him, cackling, shrieking, laughing, with such a din as the little loon never heard in his life before; and he would go off in the midst of them, telling them, no doubt, what a mighty thing it was to come down from so high and not break his neck.

A little later in the fall I saw those same loons do an astonishing thing. For several evenings they had been keeping up an unusual racket in a quiet bay, out of sight of my camp. I asked Simmo what he thought they were doing.—"O, I don' know, playin' game, I guess, jus' like one boy. Hukweem do dat sometime, wen he not hungry," said Simmo, going on with his bean-cooking. That excited my curiosity; but when I reached the bay it was too dark to see what they were playing.

One evening, when I was fishing at the inlet, the racket was different from any I had heard before. There would be an interval of perfect silence, broken suddenly by wild yelling; then the ordinary loon talk

Hukweem the Night Voice.

for a few minutes, and another silence, broken by a shriller outcry. That meant that something unusual was going on, so I left the trout, to find out about it.

When I pushed my canoe through the fringe of water-grass on the point nearest the loons, they were scattered in a long line, twelve or fifteen of them, extending from the head of the bay to a point nearly opposite me. At the other end of the line two loons were swimming about, doing something which I could not make out. Suddenly the loon talk ceased. There may have been a signal given, which I did not hear. Anyway, the two loons faced about at the same moment and came tearing down the line, using wings and feet to help in the race. The upper loons swung in behind them as they passed, so as to watch the finish better; but not a sound was heard till they passed my end of the line in a close, hard race, one scarcely a yard ahead of the other, when such a yelling began as I never heard before. All the loons gathered about the two swimmers; there was much cackling and crying, which grew gradually quieter; then they began to string out in another long line, and two more racers took their places at one end of it. By that time it was almost dark, and I broke up the race trying to get nearer in my canoe so as to watch things better.

Twice since then I have heard from summer campers of their having seen loons racing across a lake. I have no doubt it is a frequent pastime with the birds when the summer cares for the young are ended, and autumn days are mellow, and fish are plenty, and there are long hours just for fun together, before Hukweem moves southward for the hard solitary winter life on the sea-coast.

Of all the loons that cried out to me in the night, or shared the summer lakes with me, only one ever gave me the opportunity of watching at close quarters. It was on a very wild lake, so wild that no one had ever visited it before in summer, and a mother loon felt safe in leaving the open shore, where she generally nests, and placing her eggs on a bog at the head of a narrow bay. I found them there a day or two after my arrival.

I used to go at all hours of the day, hoping the mother would get used to me and my canoe, so that I could watch her later, teaching her little ones; but her wildness was unconquerable. Whenever I came in sight of the nest-bog, with only the loon's neck and head visible, standing up very straight and still in the grass, I would see her slip from the nest, steal away through the green cover to a deep place, and glide under water without leaving a ripple. Then, looking sharp over the side into the clear water, I would get a glimpse of her, just a gray streak with a string of silver bubbles, passing deep and swift under my canoe. So she went through the opening, and appeared far out in the lake, where she would swim back and forth, as if fishing, until I went away. As I never disturbed her nest, and always paddled away soon, she thought undoubtedly that she had fooled me, and that I knew nothing about her or her nest.

Then I tried another plan. I lay down in my canoe, and had Simmo paddle me up to the nest. While the loon was out on the lake, hidden by the grassy shore, I went and sat on a bog, with a friendly alder bending over me, within twenty feet of the nest, which was in plain sight. Then Simmo paddled away, and Hukweem came back without the slightest suspicion. As I had supposed, from the shape of the nest, she did not sit on her two eggs; she sat on the bog instead, and gathered them close to her side with her wing. That was all the brooding they had, or needed; for within a week there were two bright little loons to watch instead of the eggs.

After the first success I used to go alone and, while the mother bird was out on the lake, would pull my canoe up in the grass, a hundred yards or so below the nest. From here I entered the alders and made my way to the bog, where I could watch Hukweem at my leisure. After a long wait she would steal into the bay very shyly, and after much fear and circumspection glide up to the canoe. It took a great deal of looking and listening to convince her that it was harmless, and that I was not hiding near in the grass. Once convinced, however, she would come direct to the nest; and I had the satisfaction at last of watching a loon at close quarters.

She would sit there for hours — never sleeping apparently, for her eye was always bright — preening herself, turning her head slowly, so as to watch on all sides, snapping now and then at an obtrusive fly, all in utter unconsciousness that I was just behind her, watching every movement. Then, when I had enough, I would steal away along a caribou path, and push off quietly in my canoe without looking back. She saw me, of course, when I entered the canoe, but not once did she leave the nest. When I reached the open lake, a little searching with my glass always showed me her head there in the grass, still turned in my direction apprehensively.

I had hoped to see her let the little ones out of their hard shell, and see them first take the water; but that was too much to expect. One day I heard them whistling in the eggs; the next day, when I came, there was nothing to be seen on the nest-bog. I feared that something had heard their whistling and put an untimely end to the young Hukweems while mother bird was away. But when she came back, after a more fearful survey than usual of the old bark canoe, two downy little fellows came bobbing to meet her out of the grass, where she had hidden them and told them to stay till she came back.

It was a rare treat to watch them at their first feeding, the little ones all eagerness, bobbing about in the delight of eating and the wonder of the new great world, the mother all tenderness and watchfulness. Hukweem had never looked to me so noble before. This great wild mother bird, moving ceaselessly with marvelous grace about her little ones, watching their play with exquisite fondness, and watching the great dangerous world for their sakes, now chiding them gently, now drawing near to touch them with her strong bill, or to rub their little cheeks with hers, or just to croon over them in an ecstasy of that wonderful mother love which makes the summer wilderness beautiful, — in ten minutes she upset all my theories, and won me altogether, spite of what I had heard and seen of her destructiveness on the fishing grounds. After all, why should she not fish as well as I?

And then began the first lessons in swimming and hiding and diving, which I had waited so long to see.

Later I saw her bring little fish, which she had slightly wounded, turn them loose in shallow water, and with a sharp cluck bring the young loons out of their hiding, to set them chasing and diving wildly for their own dinners. But before that happened there was almost a tragedy.

One day, while the mother was gone fishing, the little ones came out of their hiding among the grasses, and ventured out some distance into the bay. It was their first journey alone into the world; they were full of the wonder and importance of it. Suddenly, as I watched, they began to dart about wildly, moving with astonishing rapidity for such little fellows, and whistling loudly. From the bank above, a swift ripple had cut out into the water between them and the only bit of bog with which they were familiar. Just behind the ripple were the sharp nose and the beady eyes of Musquash, who is always in some mischief of this kind. In one of his prowlings he had discovered the little brood; now he was manœuvering craftily to keep the frightened youngsters moving till they should be tired out, while he himself crept carefully between them and the shore.

Musquash knows well that when a young loon, or a

shelldrake, or a black duck, is caught in the open like that, he always tries to get back where his mother hid him when she went away. That is what the poor little fellows were trying to do now, only to be driven back and kept moving wildly by the muskrat, who lifted himself now and then from the water, and wiggled his ugly jaws in anticipation of the feast. He had missed the eggs in his search; but young loon would be better, and more of it.—"There you are!" he snapped viciously, lunging at the nearest loon, which flashed under water and barely escaped.

I had started up to interfere, for I had grown fond of the little wild things whose growth I had watched from the beginning, when a great splashing began on my left, and I saw the old mother bird coming like a fury. She was half swimming, half flying, tearing over the water at a great pace, a foamy white wake behind her.—"Now, you little villain, take your medicine. It's coming; it's coming," I cried excitedly, and dodged back to watch. But Musquash, intent on his evil doing (he has no need whatever to turn flesh-eater), kept on viciously after the exhausted little ones, paying no heed to his rear.

Twenty yards away the mother bird, to my great astonishment, flashed out of sight under water. What could it mean! But there was little time to wonder. Suddenly a catapult seemed to strike the muskrat from beneath and lift him clear from the water. With a tremendous rush and sputter Hukweem came out beneath him, her great pointed bill driven through to his spine. Little need of my help now. With another straight hard drive, this time at eye and brain, she flung him aside disdainfully and rushed to her shivering little ones, questioning, chiding, praising them, all in the same breath, fluttering and cackling low in an hysteric wave of tenderness. Then she swam twice around the dead muskrat and led her brood away from the place.

Perhaps it was to one of those same little ones that I owe a service for which I am more than grateful. It was in September, when I was at a lake ten miles away — the same lake into which a score of frolicking young loons gathered before moving south, and swam a race or two for my benefit. I was lost one day, hopelessly lost, in trying to make my way from a wild little lake where I had been fishing, to the large lake where my camp was. It was late afternoon. To avoid the long hard tramp down a river, up which I had come in the early morning, I attempted to cut across through unbroken forest without a compass. Traveling through a northern forest in summer is desperately hard work. The moss is ankle deep, the

Hukweem the Night Voice.

underbrush thick; fallen logs lie across each other in hopeless confusion, through and under and over which one must make his laborious way, stung and pestered by hordes of black flies and mosquitoes. So that, unless you have a strong instinct of direction, it is almost impossible to hold your course without a compass, or a bright sun, to guide you.

I had not gone half the distance before I was astray. The sun was long obscured, and a drizzling rain set in, without any direction whatever in it by the time it reached the underbrush where I was. I had begun to make a little shelter, intending to put in a cheerless night there, when I heard a cry, and looking up caught a glimpse of Hukweem speeding high over the tree-tops. Far down on my right came a faint answering cry, and I hastened in its direction, making an Indian compass of broken twigs as I went along. Hukweem was a young loon, and was long in coming down. The crying ahead grew louder. Stirred up from their day rest by his arrival, the other loons began their sport earlier than usual. The crying soon became almost continuous, and I followed it straight to the lake.

Once there, it was a simple matter to find the river and my old canoe waiting patiently under the alders in the gathering twilight. Soon I was afloat again, with a sense of unspeakable relief that only one can appreciate who has been lost and now hears the ripples sing under him, knowing that the cheerless woods lie behind, and that the camp-fire beckons beyond yonder point. The loons were hallooing far away, and I went over — this time in pure gratitude — to see them again. But my guide was modest and vanished post-haste into the mist the moment my canoe appeared.

Since then, whenever I hear Hukweem in the night, or hear others speak of his unearthly laughter, I think of that cry over the tree-tops, and the thrilling answer far away. And the sound has a ring to it, in my ears, that it never had before. Hukweem the Night Voice found me astray in the woods, and brought me safe to a snug camp. — That is a service which one does not forget in the wilderness.

GLOSSARY OF INDIAN NAMES.

Cheplahgan, *chep-lâh'-gan*, the bald eagle.
Chigwooltz, *chig-wooltz'*, the bullfrog.
Clôte Scarpe, a legendary hero, like Hiawatha, of the Northern Indians. Pronounced variously, Clote Scarpe, Groscap, Gluscap, etc.
Hukweem, *huk-weem'*, the great northern diver, or loon.
Ismaques, *iss-mâ-ques'*, the fish-hawk.
Kagax, *kăg'-ăx*, the weasel.
Killooleet, *kil'-loo-leet*, the white-throated sparrow.
Kookooskoos, *koo-koo-skoos'*, the great horned owl.
Lhoks, *locks*, the panther.
Malsun, *măl'-sun*, the wolf.
Meeko, *meek'-ō*, the red squirrel.
Megaleep, *meg'-â-leep*, the caribou.
Milicete, *mil'-ĭ-cete*, the name of an Indian tribe; written also Malicete.
Moktaques, *mok-tâ'-ques*, the hare.
Mooween, *moo-ween'*, the black bear.
Nemox, *nĕm'-ox*, the fisher.
Pekquam, *pek-wăm'*, the fisher.
Seksagadagee, *sek'-sâ-gā-dâ'-gee*, the grouse.
Tookhees, *tôk'-hees*, the wood mouse.
Upweekis, *up-week'-iss*, the Canada lynx.

CPSIA information can be obtained
at www.ICGtesting.com
Printed in the USA
LVHW110247301020
670250LV00001B/26

9 781443 779814